The only mistake Stacy had made was agreeing to have anything more to do with Graydon Payne.

Her thoughts about him were already too tender, too intimate, to be rational. The more time she spent with him, the greater the risk she might forget her place, might convince herself to overlook the danger inherent in falling in love with a man like Gray.

Stacy caught her breath. A tremor of awareness came alive in her soul. Softhearted idiot that she was, she'd fallen head over heels in love with the one man who was everything she'd always sworn she'd avoid! *Now what?* she asked herself.

The answer came easily. *Now nothing.* Graydon Payne was never going to learn how she felt about him.

Books by Valerie Hansen

Love Inspired

The Wedding Arbor #84
The Troublesome Angel #103

VALERIE HANSEN

was thirty when she awoke to the presence of the Lord in her life and turned to Jesus. In the years that followed, she worked with young children, both in church and secular environments. She also raised a family of her own and played foster mother to a wide assortment of furred and feathered critters.

Married to her high school sweetheart since age seventeen, she now lives in an old farmhouse she and her husband renovated with their own hands. She loves to hike the wooded hills behind the house and reflect on the marvelous turn her life has taken. Not only is she privileged to reside among the loving, accepting folks in the breathtakingly beautiful Ozark Mountains of Arkansas, she also gets to share her personal faith by telling the stories of her heart for Steeple Hill's Love Inspired line.

Life doesn't get much better that that!

The Troublesome Angel
Valerie Hansen

Published by Steeple Hill Books™

STEEPLE HILL BOOKS

**Steeple
Hill™**

ISBN 0-373-87109-0

THE TROUBLESOME ANGEL

Visit us at www.steeplehill.com

Printed in U.S.A.

The
Troublesome Angel
Valerie Hansen

Published by Steeple Hill Books™

STEEPLE HILL BOOKS

Steeple
Hill™

ISBN 0-373-87109-0

THE TROUBLESOME ANGEL

Copyright © 2000 by Valerie Whisenand

Visit us at www.steeplehill.com

Printed in U.S.A.

Trust in the Lord with all thine heart and lean not unto thine own understanding. In all thy ways acknowledge Him and He shall direct thy paths.
—*Proverbs* 3:5-6

Thanks to my wonderful prayer partners
in the Seekers Sunday School class and
to all the other faithful Christian friends
who bless me by simply being themselves.
And a special thanks to Joe, the love of my life,
who volunteers to cook dinner when I'm busy
writing. Contrary to popular belief, he does *not* do
it because I get so engrossed in my work that I
forget what's on the stove and burn everything. He
does it because he loves me, and supports me…and
he knows we'd *both* starve to death if he didn't!
Thanks, honey.

Chapter One

Stacy Lucas couldn't help praying the same thing over and over. "Please, Father, guide my steps and let me be in time. Please, Father…"

Barely two hours had passed since she'd received the emergency call. That was a plus. It would have been even better if she'd been at home in Cave City, instead of leading a search-and-rescue seminar hundreds of miles away. The quicker she went to work after a person was discovered missing, the greater the likelihood of success.

She focused her thoughts on the lost child as the small plane circled lower over the lush green hills of the Arkansas Ozarks, preparing to land. The scared little girl would probably hide. Most of them did. That was why Stacy's trained tracking dogs were so essential.

Her friends, Angela and Judy, both rushed across the tarmac to welcome her with hugs as soon as she climbed down out of the Cessna plane. They were babbling so anxiously they drowned each other out.

"Whoa. Take it easy, you two." Stacy stepped back and held up her hands. "Everything'll be fine. You'll see. Just give me a chance to get the dogs out of their crates and we can get started. You have no idea how worried I was when I realized it was *your* campground I was being sent to."

"We didn't want to bother you. Honest, we didn't," Angela told her. "Especially since—"

"Hey, don't apologize. I'm glad to be here. When all this is over, we'll have to catch up on old times."

She turned back to the plane and retrieved her gear from the cargo area while she watched the pilot and another man unload her dogs in their lightweight traveling kennels.

As soon as both dog boxes were safely on the ground, Stacy concentrated on her worried friends. "I'll want to know everything about the missing girl. Even the stuff you don't think is important. You can fill me in while we drive back to your place, okay?"

"It isn't going to be that easy," Angela warned.

"Why not?" Stacy was releasing her older search-and-rescue dog, Lewis, from his portable kennel. The half-grown pup, Clark, whined and barked to be let out. As soon as she had both dogs secured on leashes, she looked to her lifelong friends for an answer.

Angela Gardino was short and dark-haired. Blond Judy McKenna was the tallest of the three. Neither seemed eager to fill her in. Stacy frowned. "Well, guys?"

"Because of *him*." Judy nodded toward the Spring River Campground van parked at the edge of the tarmac.

Stacy shaded her eyes and peered. Tinted windows kept her from seeing inside. "Who is it?"

"The kid's uncle." Angela's voice was strained. "You'll never guess who he turned out to be."

"Suppose you just tell me."

Angela shook her dark curls and looked to Judy for moral support. "You do it."

"Oh, sure. Hang this on me." Judy bent, patted the eager dogs to stall for time, then straightened with a sigh. "Tell you what. Why don't we all go over to the van and let you see for yourself?"

Stacy was getting exasperated. "Look, is there a little girl lost in the woods, or not?"

"Oh, there is, all right," Angela grumbled.

"Then what are we standing around talking for? Every minute counts." Stacy slung her pack over one shoulder. "Give me a hand with the dogs' crates, will you?"

The other two women were already lifting the

cages by themselves. "We'll get these," Judy insisted. "You go on ahead."

"Okay. Just hurry up." Leading the way to the van, Stacy had no trouble attributing most of her old friends' obvious nervousness to the distressing situation of having a helpless child lost from their campground. Thank goodness the local authorities had had the good sense to call in a team of search dogs *before* the situation deteriorated.

She was barely twenty feet from the beige van when its sliding side door opened and a tall man stepped out. A baseball cap and sunglasses shaded most of his face. The rest of him was dressed far too formally for a trek in the woods, let alone camping. His suit was neatly pressed, his shoes obviously expensive. Something about his bearing reminded her of someone. Who?

The man raised his head. Dark glasses still masked his eyes, and yet... That strong chin! That arrogant mouth! That cynical expression!

Stacy's breath caught. Her stomach knotted. Her eyes widened. *Graydon Payne, of all people!* No wonder Angela and Judy hadn't wanted to tell her!

"Oh, dear God," she whispered. "What have I done to deserve *this?*"

Sensing her sudden apprehension, Lewis bristled and growled at the man. Clark, however, seemed oblivious to anything but the exciting chance to meet a new person.

Stacy expertly controlled both dogs as she approached.

The imposing man frowned. ".What are *you* doing here?"

"I'll be coordinating the search efforts for a missing little girl." She squared her shoulders proudly beneath her insulated jacket. "It's what I do now."

"For a living?" He sounded incredulous.

"Part-time, yes," Stacy said. "I suppose that surprises you, doesn't it?"

"It floors me."

"Good." She dropped her pack at his feet. "Stow that carefully, then help Judy and Angela load the dog crates in the back, will you?"

"I beg your pardon?"

Stacy couldn't help smiling. It had been years since pompous, arrogant Graydon Payne had done his best to ruin her life. She'd thought she'd never see him again. Now, here he was, apparently in need of her services, and it was a joy to be able to turn the tables and order him around for a change.

She pointed to the wire cages. "Those fold up. Lay them flat behind the back seat and let's get going. We don't want to waste precious time."

That statement seemed to jar him into action. He strode to the rear of the van and helped Judy and Angela with the cages. Stacking them as Stacy had instructed, he slammed the rear doors and quickly followed the others around to the front of the vehicle.

To his chagrin, Stacy and her rescue dogs had climbed in ahead of him and were taking up most of the available bench seat in the center. The camp-ground owners had already hopped into the two front bucket seats, leaving Graydon no choice but to sit by the panting canines. And Stacy Lucas.

Enjoying his obvious discomfiture, Stacy didn't try to control Clark's exuberance as much as she might have under other circumstances. The golden retriever-lab crossbreed wiggled happily at Gray-don's feet for a few seconds, then rose up and plopped his big paws into the man's lap as he lunged to lick his face.

Graydon's candid, "Oof!" almost made Stacy giggle. She knew this mission was a serious one—they all were—but humor often relieved the terrible tension associated with looking for missing people. And if ever there was a good reason to laugh in the midst of a potentially perilous situation, this had to be it. Pretentious Graydon Payne, the man who had once told her to leave his brother, Mark, alone because her kind didn't belong in their elevated social circles, was getting his face thoroughly licked by a dog!

"I think he likes you," Stacy wisecracked. "Although I can't for the life of me see why. I thought he was smarter than that."

"Very funny. I wish he wasn't quite so affectionate. Call him off, will you?"

"Oh, okay. Clark. Down." The dog obeyed immediately.

"Thanks." Graydon dusted off his hands, then brushed at his dark slacks. "He's shedding."

"Probably. You'll be glad to hear we haven't been crashing through any patches of poison ivy lately, though."

"Oh, good." His tone was cynical.

Stacy got down to business. "So, the missing child is your niece?"

"In a manner of speaking."

"That sounds like typical Payne reasoning. Is she, or isn't she?"

"She will be. She's being adopted into the family."

It took Stacy only an instant to remember that Graydon's sister, Rosalie, already had children. Which probably meant the missing little girl was to be Mark's new daughter. Therefore, Mark must have married. That assumption lay like a stone on her heart...until she thought about what had happened and clearly saw the Lord's hand in shaping her life.

Graydon watched her, assessing her reactions. It was hard to believe this was the same Stacy Lucas he'd once known. That girl had been an underachiever. All she'd had on her mind was marrying his brother and gaining the security that came with the Payne money and their good name. He'd have sworn there wasn't an altruistic bone in her body. And *now* look at her.

He cast her a sidelong glance. In many ways she was the same, with long, golden-brown hair and eyes the color of a summer sky. But her attitude and bearing were totally different from what he remembered. She'd been shy and unassuming when Mark had brought her home to meet the family. This Stacy Lucas was self-assured, poised and evidently well thought of in her profession. He just hoped she didn't hold a grudge when it came to doing what she and her dogs were trained for.

"Listen, Stacy, I'm sorry if…"

She waved her hand to dismiss his unfinished sentence, turned away and stared out the window. "There's no need to apologize, Mr. Payne. You and I have had our differences but that's all in the past. Actually, Mark did me a favor."

"He did?"

"Yes. If we'd married back then, as I'd hoped, I might never have followed my heart and become involved with search and rescue. I've wanted to do this job ever since I was a kid. In a roundabout way, I guess you could say I owe you and your family for my rewarding career."

Closing her eyes for an instant she had a fleeting flashback to the plane crash that had made her an orphan when she was barely ten years old.

Unconsciously, she rubbed the top of her thigh through her jeans. Nowadays, hardly anyone noticed the slight limp which was her only tangible tie to that awful night. In her memory, however, fragments of the incident replayed almost daily, especially when she was on assignment.

She felt a familiar nudge at her knee. Lewis laid his furry chin in her lap, begging her to scratch his ears. Not to be outdone, long-haired, golden Clark wiggled in between her and Graydon, trying his best to displace his comrade.

Stacy smiled down at them. "You boys are ready to work, aren't you?" Lewis stared up at her as if understanding every word, his tail thumping against the wall of the van.

Impatient, Clark wasted no more time vying for her attention. Instead, he turned his efforts back to the man seated next to his mistress.

"Oh, no. Not again." Graydon caught the dog's front feet in midair and held him off. "Down!" To his surprise, Clark sank back to the floor as he was told. "Well, well. What do you know? Maybe he really does like me."

Stacy was going to say, "He also likes to steal garbage out of the trash when I'm not looking," then decided against voicing the thought. There was no use goading her former nemesis. Graydon Payne might live up to his name and be a real *pain*, but he was still a member of the public she'd sworn to serve. What was past was past. The important thing was the missing little girl, she reminded herself, again. All else was trivial.

Even the old scars on her broken heart.

When Stacy arrived at the campground, she was met with utter chaos. The local sheriff greeted her solemnly as he shook her hand. "I'm sure glad to see you, ma'am. It's been a long time since we've needed you."

"Hello, Frank. I'm glad I was available. You ready to fill me in?"

"Not much to tell. We've got a real mess out there in the woods, a bunch of folks beatin' the bushes, hollering at each other and gettin' nowhere fast."

"That's normal," Stacy said. "Where've you set up your command post?"

"Over here." He led the way.

Stacy sensed Graydon following. The fine hairs on the back of her neck prickled a primitive warning. What a jolt it had been to encounter him again! And how odd to sense that he was truly concerned for the missing six-year-old. The Graydon Payne she'd met when she was dating Mark had seemed totally oblivious to the needs and concerns of others.

Ignoring his formidable presence hovering directly behind her, she greeted the other searchers with a polite, businesslike nod and immediately launched into her standard instruction speech. They were to cover designated quadrants of the forest, reporting in at set intervals and notifying the command post before deviating from their assigned territory for any reason. Once each team had finished the first wave of searching, they'd be given orders as to what to do next.

"I'll take my dogs and sweep out from the last place the girl was seen," Stacy concluded. "I'll be the only one moving in random directions. Is that clear?"

The men nodded. Pointing to the map, Stacy quickly gave out their assignments, then led them in silent prayer before she dismissed them. They moved away in groups of two. Only the sheriff remained to man the command post.

"I'm coming with you," Graydon announced.

Hearing his deep voice so close behind her gave Stacy a start. She whirled. "Thanks, but no thanks." A faint tremor in her hands was the only thing that betrayed her nervousness. "I work alone."

"Not this time, you don't."

She glared up at him, fists on her hips, stance firm and wide, radiating authority. Her dog spoiled the image when he lunged to one side and almost pulled her off her feet.

Graydon was frowning. "I'm going. That's all there is to it. If you don't let me walk with you, I'll just follow anyway. Which would you rather have?"

"Neither. But I don't suppose that was one of the choices, was it?"

"No."

"You'll ruin your good clothes."

"I have others."

"I'll bet you do." She pressed her lips into a thin line. Reasoning with a stubborn man like him was impossible.

Clark gave another mighty jerk on the leash. Teenage dogs were usually incorrigible and this one was no exception. He was twice as headstrong as Lewis had been at the same age.

Stacy's quick mind assessed the situation. Maybe there was a way around her dilemma after all. If Graydon went along with her plan, she'd have Clark out of the way so Lewis could work, unhindered. If he refused, she'd have *him* out of the way. Either choice made her the clear winner.

She extended her left hand, Clark's leash held tightly in her fist. "Okay, take this. Borrow some survival gear and meet me back here in five minutes. I'm putting you in charge of this dog."

"Me?" Graydon's scowl deepened.

"Why not? You said he likes you."

"Yes, but... What if I make a mistake? I don't know anything about search and rescue."

"Then you and the dog are about even," Stacy countered. "He doesn't either." She heard the sheriff chuckle in the background.

Graydon snatched the leash out of her hand. "That's comforting."

"I thought you'd like it." She met his challenging gaze boldly. "See if you can find something else the little girl touched recently, preferably an item of her clothing. Bring it with you when you come back. Remember, five minutes, tops. After that, I'll be gone."

To avoid any more argumentative conversation, she turned her back on Graydon Payne and concentrated solely on the sheriff. "Now, Frank, what other evidence have you turned up and what else can you tell me before I leave?"

Graydon returned within three minutes, much to Stacy's chagrin. Over his suit he wore a bright-orange, hooded sweatshirt, the kind hunters used to keep from being confused with their prey. He reached into the pocket of the coat and brought out a small, pink glove with white-and-brown bunnies knit into the pattern on the cuff. "Will this do? I found it at the edge of camp."

Stacy recognized it as the mate to the plastic-wrapped glove the sheriff had passed on to her. "Why didn't you give that to Frank?"

"He has the other one. In all the confusion I forgot I'd stuffed this one in my pocket."

"You're sure it's hers?"

"Positive. I bought these gloves and a matching jacket for Missy—Melissa—when I heard Mark and Candace were taking her camping. They said she loved them...wore them all the time, even at home."

A twinge of mild regret stirred in Stacy's heart. So, Mark was married, just as she'd figured. To her surprise, the thought didn't linger long enough to make her melancholy. There was no time for self-pity. A poor, frightened child was wandering alone in the wilderness, probably crying, freezing and hungry. That was all that mattered.

She looked to Graydon. "Okay. Show me exactly where you found the glove. We'll start there."

"It was over by the rest rooms, on a path that leads into the forest." He pointed. "That way."

"And you're sure she left of her own accord?"

"Positive. Several people saw her go."

"Okay." Taking the glove, Stacy held it for Lewis to smell, then guided him in the direction Graydon had indicated. It didn't take him long to strike a trail, put his nose to the ground and start into the woods at a fast pace.

"Good boy, Lewis. Go on! Find her!" Adrenaline surged through Stacy, sharpening her already keen senses. *Praise God,* the trail was still warm so the chances of finding the child were very good, especially with a competent tracking dog like Lewis on the job.

He was the calm, sensible one of the pair, the one whose head was always clear, whose canine judgment she trusted implicitly. Clark, on the other hand, was a clown in a dog suit. It was hard to believe they were half brothers.

Which reminded her... Glancing over her shoulder, Stacy caught a glimpse of Graydon and the younger dog. They were lagging behind while Clark sniffed the base of an interesting tree. That figured. His faculties might be as good as Lewis's but his instincts pertaining to a search were sorely lacking. Until he learned to prioritize, he was next to useless as a rescue dog, no matter how well he could find hidden items in the course of his training.

And speaking of *useless,* she added, there was also the matter of Graydon Payne. She should never have assigned Clark to him. It would probably take her weeks to undo the damage he was doing to the poor dog's training.

She called back. "This way! Make him follow us."

"How do you expect me to do *that?*" Graydon yelled. "This dog has a mind of his own."

"Yours is supposed to be stronger," she countered. "Show him who's boss."

"*He* is, in case you haven't noticed."

Whistling, Stacy got the retriever's attention and he headed for her at a dead run, dragging the surprised man along behind him in a stumbling, sliding charge.

By the time Graydon and Clark arrived at the spot where Stacy had stood, she and Lewis were already underway again.

"You could wait for us," he shouted.

"Not when there's a child who needs me," she called back over her shoulder.

He jogged to catch up, his smooth-soled shoes slipping on the pine needle carpet as Clark pulled him along. Short of breath, he managed to gasp, "You really take this stuff seriously, don't you?"

Stacy's jaw clenched. She was used to having people question her skills, especially since she was a fairly small woman, but coming from Graydon

Payne the remark sounded even more negative than usual.

"Search and rescue is my life," she said flatly. "And I'm very good at my job."

When he answered, "I believe you," sounding totally truthful, she was temporarily speechless.

"If this had happened a month ago, before all the trees leafed out, we'd have a better chance of spotting her." Stacy paused to catch her breath and check her topographical map. The sloping, densely forested and rocky terrain had slowed Lewis's progress considerably and he seemed to have temporarily lost the child's trail.

Graydon was breathing hard, too. "We'll still be able to find Missy, won't we?"

"I hope so. It's not as cold today as it has been. That gives us a bigger window of opportunity."

"You don't sound terribly concerned."

"Don't I? Sorry." She took a drink of water from her canteen. "The truth is, I care very much. I also know that an emotional approach to a case like this often leads to critical mistakes. That's the last thing we want. If Lewis doesn't find her soon, I'll call in other handlers and add more dogs to the search party."

"Good." Graydon eyed the canteen, held out his hand. "I could use a swallow of that."

"Where's yours? I told you to get survival gear before we left camp." For the first time, she noticed he wasn't carrying a backpack.

"You gave me so little time I didn't have a chance to do more than grab this coat out of somebody's truck," he alibied, patting the front pockets of the bright-orange hunting jacket. "I've got a candy bar in here but that's about all."

"Terrific. I knew I shouldn't have let you come along."

Bestowing a slight, lopsided smile on his companion and trying to look suitably contrite, Graydon held out the candy bar. "Trade you half of this for a drink of water?"

"I have my own food. Thanks, anyway."

"You're not going to make this easy for me, are you?"

"Nope."

His smile grew. "You *have* changed."

Stacy looked up at him and nodded. "Mister, you have no idea."

Chapter Two

Graydon slipped the candy back into his pocket. "Please?"

"Is this your idea of begging? Sheesh!"

"I'm not used to it. That's the best I can do. Come on. Be a sport and give me a drink." He reached toward the canteen, freezing in midmotion when Lewis growled. "Oh-oh. Maybe I should have offered the candy to the dog."

"Don't do it. Chocolate can be toxic to dogs." Stacy couldn't help smiling as she explained, "Lewis is my official protector. When you got too close, he let you know how things stood, but I don't think he'd go so far as to actually bite you."

"How comforting."

Relenting, she held out the canteen. "Here. Just don't drink too much. We need to save some for Melissa when we find her."

Raising one dark brow, Graydon kept an eye on the defensive animal at her feet, took a swallow and handed back the canteen. "Do you think we're close?"

"I can't be sure. Lewis was acting confused when I stopped. He's either lost the trail or it's become complicated because the child doubled back."

Graydon cocked his head toward the far end of the taut leash he was still holding. The younger dog was busy sniffing dirt, sprigs of grass and nearby insects. "This one acted kind of funny by that dead tree at the bottom of the hill. Do you think he might have caught a whiff of Missy's trail?"

"Clark?" Stacy huffed in disgust. "I doubt it. He's about as aware of what's going on as these rocks we're standing on."

"Then why bring him?"

"It's good training. If I don't expose young dogs to real working conditions and the hardships of the trail, I won't be sure I can rely on them when the time finally comes for them to function alone. Clark will learn a lot by watching Lewis. I hope."

"Lewis and Clark? Oh, I get it." Graydon made a sarcastic sound deep in his throat. "Cute."

Stacy wasn't about to let him antagonize her. "Look, Mr. Payne. I didn't come out here to defend my training methods or my dogs. I'm here to find a lost child. Nothing else counts. So if you want to waste time arguing, I suggest you go back to camp and pick on somebody else.''

Frustrated, he ran his fingers through his thick, dark hair, pushing it back off his forehead. ''I didn't realize I was picking on you. I'm sorry if that's the way it sounded. I guess I'm more worried about Missy than I thought.''

Stacy was instantly penitent. ''Of course you are. It's perfectly natural. I shouldn't have snapped at you. I'm sorry, too.''

One corner of his mouth lifted in a half smile. ''Okay. That's decided.''

''What is?''

''That we're both sorry excuses for sympathetic human beings. Now, tell me the truth. What are our chances of finding Missy?'' He couldn't bring himself to add, *alive.*

Stacy heard the unspoken question in his tone. ''I think they're very good.'' She laid her hand lightly on his arm to comfort him as she spoke. ''Kids tend to live in the moment rather than plan ahead, like finding water to drink or a place to keep warm at night, the way an adult might. They mostly wander aimlessly at first, then hunker down to sleep when they run out of energy, which makes them doubly hard to find unless a rescuer has a dog with a good nose and strong instincts.''

''A dog like Lewis.''

''Yes.'' Stacy reached down to give the animal a pat. She owed her own life to a dog that had led a search party to her when she'd been lost and nearly frozen to death. No matter how long she lived or how hard she worked, she knew she'd never be able to repay that debt. She also knew she'd never stop trying. It was her job. The career that God had arranged for her. At times like this, it was crucial to remember that the Lord was in charge. Of everything. Which might mean…

Pensive, she looked up at Graydon. "Tell me again. Where was Clark sniffing when you thought he was acting funny?"

"Down there. By the big, dead oak. Do you think…?"

"Maybe. It's worth a try."

She stopped him when he started to lead the way. "Wait. Let Lewis and me go first so we don't muddy up the scent anymore than we already have."

Graydon nodded and pulled back. Restraining Clark, he watched Stacy make her way down the slope. There was quite a contrast between the no-nonsense persona she presented to the world and the empathetic part of her character, wasn't there? She'd tried to keep her sensitive nature hidden but he'd sensed it from the moment he'd seen her again. The truth dwelt in her eyes, betrayed a tender-hearted spirit. Stacy Lucas cared. Deeply. And he admired her for it.

Coming to his senses, Graydon berated himself for letting his attention wander. The only thing he should be concentrating on at a time like this was finding Missy…before it was too late. His stomach knotted. No way was he going to let anything happen to that darling little girl. She must be so scared, so alone.

Graydon knew what it was like to be totally alone, even in a crowd. He'd had a whole lifetime to adjust to the feelings of emotional isolation he'd battled ever since he was a boy.

Clark was so eager to join Lewis that he couldn't stand still. He whined and lunged against the restraint of the leash, then began to run in circles around the man who was holding him back.

Looking down the hill, Graydon saw Lewis and Stacy in the distance. The dog had taken off again, pulling his leash taut and making Stacy run to keep up. He must have struck the trail!

Gathering the braided nylon lead in his hand, Graydon kept Clark on a short tether so he could extricate himself from the tangled loops the dog had made around the calves of his legs.

"Okay, okay. I get the idea," he grumbled. "Just a minute, stupid. You're the one who got us all fouled up like this, not me."

As he bent to step out of the last confining coil of nylon, Clark lunged. The leash tightened. Graydon hit the ground with a thud, feet in the air!

The enthusiastic dog immediately jumped atop his chest, licking his face with delight.

"Stop that! Down!" Spitting dry, crumbled leaves and muttering under his breath, Graydon pushed the friendly pup away and scrambled to his feet. Thank goodness Stacy Lucas hadn't been close enough to see him knocked down!

Anxious, he peered down the hill. She and her dog were still in sight!

"Okay, you dunderhead," he told Clark. "Let's get going before we lose your mommy."

The dog wagged his plume of a tail and looked up at the man as if he understood every word.

Stacy glanced over her shoulder to make sure her so-called partner reached the bottom of the steep hill safely. Clark was casting left and right, sniffing the air, just the way a rescue dog was supposed to. Would wonders never cease! Maybe she'd been right to keep training him after all.

Shouting, "Over here," and waving her arm wildly so Graydon could see where she was going, she plunged into a thick stand of oak and cedar, following Lewis. The dog immediately began whining and scratching at a pile of dried leaves and twigs beneath the largest tree.

"Good boy, Lewis! Good boy!" He began to dig more frantically. Brown refuse flew. Stacy got a glimpse of bright pink. The jacket! It had to be.

"Oh, please Lord, let her be here," she prayed softly. "And let her be all right."

Approaching, she tightened up the leash and ordered Lewis to sit. "Melissa? Is that you?"

There was no answer.

Stacy crouched down, reached out her hand, and brushed off the exposed arm of the jacket. "Melissa? It's okay, honey. I've come to take you back."

The child bolted out from under the leaves and clambered away with a shriek. Startled, Stacy rocked back on her heels and nearly fell over backward.

She was alive! Stacy's breath left her in a whoosh of pure relief. She sank to her knees, her arms around Lewis, her prayers of thanks so heartfelt they were wordless. Tears blurred her vision.

"It's okay, Melissa," she said, fighting to speak calmly. "We won't hurt you. The dog is real friendly. He helped me find you. Isn't that nice?"

The tremulous reply came as a sobbed, "No!"

That surprised Stacy. She'd had disoriented adults try to refuse a rescue but she'd never seen a child do it. They were usually so glad to be found they were no trouble at all.

Melissa faced her, blue eyes wide and frightened, long, strawberry-blond hair matted with twigs, leaves and dirt. Tears left muddy streaks as they trickled down her cheeks. "I don't wanna go back. Never ever." Sniffling and wiping her nose on her sleeve, she started to inch away.

"Wouldn't you like to pet my dog?" As hoped, that offer stopped the child's retreat. "He's very nice. Aren't you, Lewis? Would you like to shake hands with Missy?"

The little girl's tears ceased. "Wh-what?"

"I said, Lewis would like to shake hands with you."

"You called me Missy."

"Isn't that right?" Stacy knew she could always grab the child and take her back forcibly but she didn't want to traumatize her any more than she already was. The best thing to do would be to drag out their conversation long enough for Graydon to arrive. Then the poor, scared little girl wouldn't have to trust a stranger.

"I like people to call me Missy," she said softly.

"Then that's what I'll do," Stacy vowed. She held out her hand. "Friends?"

Before she could answer, Clark and Graydon broke through the thick stand of trees at a run, startling everyone. The instant he spotted the child he let go of the leash and opened his arms. "Missy!"

Squealing, she ran into his embrace. "Uncle Gray!"

He scooped her up and spun around in circles. Pure joy filled the clearing. The sight of the usually formal man hugging the dirty waif brought fresh tears to Stacy's eyes. This was what her job was all about.

He spoke lovingly, without reproach. "Where have you been, Missy? I was worried sick! We all were."

"I don't wanna go back to Mark's." She buried her face in his collar.

"You don't want me for an uncle?" he asked.

"Course I do."

"Well, I can't be your uncle if you aren't Mark's daughter."

She raised her head and studied him. "You can't?"

"Nope. That's how it has to be."

Stacy could tell from Missy's expression that she was thinking hard. There was no telling what kind of temporary living conditions the motherless child had been subjected to. It was natural for her to be afraid. Of everything.

Approaching them slowly, Stacy patted Missy on the back and spoke soothing words while Gray continued to hold her.

He gazed down at Stacy over the child's shoulder and mouthed, "Thank you."

"You're quite welcome." Stacy stepped away and reached for the handheld, two-way radio she carried. "I'm going to call in the good news and get everybody headed back into camp." She glanced at the sky. "We'd better get a move on, too. It'll be dark soon."

She saw Graydon close his eyes for a moment as he nodded acknowledgment. Clearly, he cared about this child. Finding her so quickly had been the first miracle. Realizing that any Payne had a loving bone in his or her body had been the second. The third would probably be getting Clark to walk calmly back to camp without taking off to chase squirrels or rabbits.

She watched her two dogs tussling while she used the radio. Lewis usually put up with Clark's exuberance with stoic grace until the pup got too pushy. Then he simply growled a warning and the younger dog backed off. Too bad people weren't that smart.

Stacy smiled to herself as she considered her impromptu helper. For a stuffy businessman in a silk suit and Italian loafers, he'd conducted himself quite well.

Of course he did, she countered. He wanted something from me. "Something I was more than happy to give," she whispered. At least this time, Graydon Payne hadn't asked her to walk away from love.

Other ecstatic searchers mobbed them as they entered the campground. Nearly everybody was shouting and cheering. Some wept.

Graydon still carried Melissa. Stacy fell back and let him precede her into the camp.

Lanterns glowed everywhere. News cameras with blinding lights illuminated the area as brightly as a summer day. Mark Payne stood in the center of the circle of well-wishers. His arm was around the shoulders of a woman who looked as if she'd just stepped out of a fashion magazine. Every dark hair was in place, her nails were long and polished, her makeup was flawless and she was smiling demurely. A perfect couple in a perfect world.

That was what bothered Stacy the most. While Graydon had shouted and run to Melissa the moment he saw her, the child's prospective parents were just standing there, waiting for her to be delivered. Like a package.

Purposely avoiding Mark, Stacy veered away from the crowd. She wasn't angry with him or sorry he'd married someone else. Not anymore. She simply had nothing relevant to say to him. Besides, her job was over. She and the dogs had done what they'd come for. Now, all she had to do was find Judy and Angela and arrange for one of them to drive her home to Cave City in the morning.

Judy met her halfway to the camp office that also doubled as living quarters. Hugging Stacy, she grinned foolishly. "Congratulations!"

"Thanks. Where's Angie?"

"She went to bed with a migraine and missed all the excitement." A wistful smile replaced the wide grin. "I thought I was going to cry like a baby when I saw that kid again. You did a great job. You're a genius."

"I don't do the sniffing, the dogs do. But thanks, anyway."

"Well, okay. So you hang out with geniuses. Hairy ones." She bent to ruffle Clark's ears, then gave Lewis a more gentle pat on the head. "This one looks kind of droopy."

"I know. He's tired. I'm going to retire him soon. He's not as young as he used to be. You'd never know it, though, when he's hot on the trail."

"Speaking of being hot on somebody's trail..." She cocked her head back toward the gathering of rescuers, reporters, cameramen and celebrants. "Look. Here comes you-know-who."

"I don't have to look," Stacy said, making a face. "It's getting so I can sense when he's around. The hair on the back of my neck prickles."

"Uh-oh. Sounds serious. Let me know if he starts to give you indigestion. That's a sure sign you're interested."

Stacy's silly expression became a grimace and she rolled her eyes to exaggerate her sentiment. "Don't be ridiculous. You know I had my fill of Payne men a long time ago."

"True. But you never know what intriguing surprises God might have in store for you." Judy leaned closer, cupped her hand around her mouth, and added, "You haven't been praying for a husband, have you?"

"Certainly not! And if I had been, Graydon Payne would be the last man—" The direction of Judy's glance and her widening grin told Stacy it was time to stop talking. Maybe past time.

She turned slowly. Graydon was smiling down at her benevolently. "Did I hear my name mentioned?"

"Not on purpose, you didn't," Stacy said, quickly changing the subject. "How's Missy doing?"

"She's too tired to cause much of a ruckus." He held out his business card. "Give me a call and I'll be glad to fill you in on her progress. In the meantime, I want to thank you for all you've done.''

''It's my job.'' Stacy took his card reluctantly.

''Nevertheless, I'd like to shake your hand.''

She had no good reason to refuse such a request. Nor was she sure why she felt so hesitant. The man had been a perfect gentleman while they'd been in the woods. Not that she'd expected any less from him. After all, he'd once told her that her social station was so far beneath his and his family's, he wouldn't be able to stoop that far down if he'd tried.

Remembering their past unhappy association brought back Stacy's professional air. She handed control of the dogs to Judy, took his hand, shook it formally, and said, ''It was my pleasure to be able to help, Mr. Payne.''

If he'd released her at that moment, she'd have been fine. Instead, however, he clasped her hand as if they were the best of friends and covered it with his other, looking at her warmly.

Stacy's pulse quickened. Short of breath, she tried to pull away. ''What are you doing?''

''Trying to show my appreciation.'' His thumb grazed her wrist, setting up a tingle that shot up her arm and did a tap dance along her spine.

''A simple 'Thank you' would suffice.''

''I don't think that's enough. You showed up here as soon as you were called and performed with great professionalism and skill. I'm indebted to you. Aren't all the people you help grateful?''

"Not so you'd notice," Stacy said truthfully. "Most of the time they're too caught up in what's happened to even realize I'm there."

Graydon continued to hold her hand. "That's too bad. You deserve more praise."

"I'm not in this business for the glory, which is why I'm trying to dodge all those reporters," she said, glancing back at the crowd. "And stop that."

"Stop what?"

"That." Stacy clasped her free hand over his and stilled his casual caress. To her surprise, he released her as if he were dropping a red-hot coal. Not only that, he looked like he might actually be blushing under his perfect tan.

"I'm sorry. I didn't realize—"

"That I'm not the impressionable girl I used to be?" She smiled coolly. "You don't owe me a thing, Mr. Payne. Neither does anyone else in your family. No one could pay me enough to cover the long hours, sweat and tears I put into my job."

"Then why do you do it?"

It would have been simple to give him a pat answer. It would also have been a sin. Stacy knew better than to pass up the chance to offer an honest statement of her faith. Such opportunities didn't come every day. They were far too precious to be wasted.

"Because I'm trying to follow God's leading for my life," she said, "to stay in His will, to be the person He expects me to be."

"That's very noble."

"No, it isn't. It's hard. And scary. And sometimes it breaks my heart." Stacy's voice softened. "If I were in charge of the universe, no one would ever fail. Or be lost. Or lonely. Or die. I don't understand why things happen the way they do. I never did. All I can do is give it my best and put my faith in Jesus."

"Even when you fail?" he asked quietly.

"Oh, yes." She looked up at him, willing him to understand. "*Especially* when I fail."

Chapter Three

By nine that night the campground had quieted down. Too tired to go home, Stacy had showered, eaten, borrowed a pink sweat suit from Judy and was sprawled in a comfy chair by the fireplace in the main cabin. Lewis and Clark both lay napping by her bare feet.

She pushed up the oversize sleeves of the sweatshirt and hugged herself. "Umm, this feels so good. Thanks again. I was in such a big hurry to get here and begin the search I came straight from the seminar in Atlanta. I wish now I'd gone home to get different clothes."

"No problem. Too bad I don't have something more your size. You should let me wake Angela and ask her."

"No way. I know what her migraines are like. She needs to sleep it off."

"You're right. So what's Plan B? Do you need to go back to Atlanta and finish up there or what?"

Stacy picked up her mug of hot cocoa, wrapped both hands around it to enjoy the warmth and took a sip. "No. I'm all done. The last of my tracking demonstrations were over by late yesterday. That's one of the reasons I was free to respond when we got your call. Everybody else is still committed to wrapping up their classes."

"I'll bet that was no accident. I was sure praying you'd be the one they sent."

"I'm glad, too. I've been so busy lately I haven't taken time for my friends. I've really missed you guys."

"We understand how it is. I'm just sorry it turned out to be the Paynes who needed your help."

Thoughtful, Stacy nodded and sighed. "Yeah. Me, too. For more reasons than one." Ever since she'd stepped off the plane and encountered Graydon she'd been feeling an uncomfortable pricking at the edges of her conscience. "I'm afraid the Lord may be trying to nudge me about something."

"Like what?" Leaning closer, Judy added, "Forgiveness?"

That insight took Stacy by surprise. Her eyes widened. "How did you know what I was thinking?"

"I didn't. But I know you. It's not like you to hold a grudge or be unfriendly toward anybody. I think it's possible the Lord threw Graydon Payne in your path to get you to face the old hostility you've hung on to for so long.''

The idea did not sit well with Stacy. Caught up in the pathos and excitement of Missy's rescue, she'd managed to temporarily set aside her intense, long-standing dislike for Graydon and his stuffy family. Now it was back.

She knew it was wrong to harbor resentment. She also knew she wasn't ready to lower her guard and give up the protection those hostile feelings provided. They were necessary for her emotional well-being.

Purposely changing the subject, Stacy said, ''I was hoping you or Angela could spare an hour or so to drive me home in the morning.''

''Sure.'' Judy relaxed, leaned back. ''Anything for a hero.''

''Cut that out. I'm not—''

The dogs perked up and stared at the door. A loud knock sounded. Lewis growled. Clark jumped up, tail wagging.

''If that's more reporters, please don't let them in.'' Stacy yawned. ''I'm too tired to make good sense.''

''Right.'' Judy's outlandish bunny slippers made a swishing sound as she padded to the door, followed closely by the younger dog. ''Who is it?''

A man's voice said, ''Special delivery for Ms. Lucas.''

''Try again,'' Judy countered. ''In case you

haven't noticed, we're in the middle of nowhere. The post office has enough trouble delivering our regular mail. No way is there a special delivery at this time of night.''

In spite of her weariness, Stacy joined her, and pressed her ear to the door. ''Who is it?''

''Santa Claus?'' the voice ventured. He waited, then tried again. ''How about Howard Hughes?''

''It's Graydon Payne,'' Stacy deduced, scowling. ''It has to be. Look how Clark's tail is wagging.'' Louder, she called, ''What do you want?''

''To give you something.''

''There's nothing you have that I want.''

''Then take it as a gift for the rescue program.''

Judy nudged her. ''He's got a point there. No use turning down a donation.''

''Slip it under the door.''

Casting her friend a disparaging glance, Judy opened the door instead. ''Come on in. Only one of us bites, and it's *not* the dogs.''

Graydon paused to lean down and greet Clark with, ''Hi, buddy. Did you miss me?'' He ruffled the dog's silky ears as he entered the cozy cabin. ''You did, didn't you? I knew we were pals.''

''Hah!'' Stacy wasn't impressed, even if her idiotic dog had chosen that particular moment to roll over on his back at the man's feet and beg to have his tummy scratched. That act of submission meant Clark trusted Graydon implicitly.

''Don't pay any attention to her,'' Judy said,

gesturing at Stacy. "She's always like this when she's dead tired."

"Grouchy?" He straightened, smiling.

"Catatonic. I've seen her practically fall asleep leaning against a tree…standing up."

"That must make quite a picture."

His wry smile and knowing gaze amused Stacy in spite of herself. "Watch for film at eleven," she quipped. "The news crews just left."

"I thought you were avoiding them."

"I don't like catching a cold, either, but some things are inevitable."

"True."

They were standing just inside the door, facing each other. Stacy's weary brain was devoid of small talk. She looked up at him, intending to close their conversation, and was astonished to note an appealing sparkle in his eyes. They were dark-brown with a golden cast, not blue, like Mark's. And his chin was more square, more masculine. Right now it was shadowed with a day's growth of beard, giving him a rugged look. It was a definite improvement.

Noting her awareness, he raised an eyebrow and raked his fingers through his thick, dark hair. "Is something wrong?"

If Stacy hadn't been so tired she might have censored her reply more carefully. Instead, she said, "Nope. I was just noticing how human you look when you're not so perfectly groomed."

"Oh, I see." He began to chuckle. "You look

different, too. Either that outfit stretched or you shrank. It makes you look like a teenager. Kind of cute.''

Blushing, Stacy refused to look away and give him the last word. ''Flattery will get you nowhere.''

''Too bad. Guess I'll have to come up with another approach the next time I want to impress you.''

''There won't be any next time,'' she countered. ''After tonight I doubt we'll ever meet again.''

He sobered. ''I suppose you're right. Which is why I stopped by.'' Reaching into the pocket of his jacket he took out a check. ''We want you to have this. Call it a reward, if you like.''

She hesitated several long seconds before giving in. ''All right. I'll take it. But only because the rescue program needs the financial support.''

''Of course.''

''I mean it. None of this is for me.''

''You don't have to convince me,'' he said quietly. ''I believe you.''

Looking up at him, she scrutinized his expression as she asked, ''Why?''

''Because I'm a Christian, too,'' Graydon said. ''And I don't lie, either.''

Her eyes widened. Their gazes locked. ''You are?''

''Does it surprise you?''

''Frankly, yes.''

Graydon laughed softly. ''You're not the only

one who was surprised, lady. It sure shocked me when it happened.''

"What did you do, get hit by lightning?'' Stacy still couldn't believe he wasn't teasing her.

"I get the feeling you don't think it's possible for me to change.''

"That's not for me to judge, one way or the other,'' she countered. "Your faith is between you and God. I'm sure Jesus knows what's really in your heart.''

"Yes, he does.'' Graydon didn't extend his hand to her this time. Instead, he turned and reached for the doorknob. Glancing back, he paused and said, "Goodbye, Stacy. And thank you.''

She barely had time to echo, "Goodbye,'' before he was gone, leaving an intangible void in his wake.

Judy's "Wow!'' filled the silence.

Startled, Stacy spun around. "I forgot you were here.''

"No kidding. I could have set off fireworks in your pockets and neither one of you would have paid the slightest bit of attention.''

"Don't be silly.''

"Okay. Have it your way.'' Judy went back to her place on the couch and sat down, patting the cushion beside her so Clark would jump up and join her. He settled down next to her immediately, his golden head on her lap.

"You're spoiling that dog,'' Stacy told her. "By

the time I undo all the bad habits you and Graydon Payne have taught him, I'll be ninety.''

"Clark seems to like him."

"The dog's a doofus."

Judy chuckled. "He's not the only one. I couldn't believe it when you asked the poor man if he'd been hit by lightning!"

"I did?" Stacy thought for a moment, trying to sort out the muddle her mind had been in ever since Graydon Payne had walked through the door. "Oh, boy. I did, didn't I?"

"Uh-huh. But he took it pretty well. I'll bet he really is a Christian."

"His family's always been big on church-going. Mark took me with him several times when we were dating."

"That's not what I mean and you know it."

Stacy did know. People didn't turn into cars when they stepped into a garage any more than they became Christians just by going to church. Warming a pew on Sunday morning might be good for your psyche, but it didn't make you a believer. Neither did living an exemplary life. She ought to know. She'd done both as a child, and been miserable until she'd given up one day and turned her future over to Jesus. But could Graydon Payne have done the same thing?

She sighed. "Oh, dear."

"What's the matter?" Judy was rhythmically stroking Clark's broad head.

"I just realized something."

"From the scrunched-up face you're making, I'd guess you aren't thrilled."

"No kidding."

"Well? Give. What's got you so dithered?"

"If that man really is a Christian, we're part of the same family—God's family."

"So?"

"So I'm supposed to love him. Accept him. I don't even *like* him!"

Laughing softly, Judy shook her head. "You sure could have fooled me."

"I don't know what to do with her," Mark said, pacing his spacious, sunken living room. "Ever since Melissa met Stacy and saw those dogs, that's all she's talked about. Candace is getting really steamed about it."

Graydon nodded. "I can understand that. She wants Missy to love her like a mother. But it's not going to happen overnight. Kids need time to adjust."

"That's what the social workers said when I called them. I just wish I could do what they've suggested." Mark cast a sidelong glance up the spiral staircase. "But Candace would kill me."

"What did they tell you to do?"

Mark fidgeted and managed to smile at his older brother in spite of his obvious apprehension. "It's not a big thing. It'd only take an afternoon. Just long enough to run down to Cave City and back."

Raising an eyebrow, Graydon studied him. Ever

since they were kids he'd been bailing Mark out of trouble, and it sounded like his baby brother wanted him to do it again. He decided to make him actually ask before he volunteered anything. The guy had to grow up sometime.

Mark cleared his throat. "You busy next week?"

"Boy, no kidding. I've been snowed under getting the city council in Conway to approve the plans for the consolidated mall project. I'll probably have to fly to Saint Louis next week, too. If I'd known how much work this development consultant job was going to be, I might have accepted Dad's offer of a vice presidency, like you."

"You did the right thing," Mark said, scowling. "Working for our father is no picnic. If it wasn't for Candace I'd probably have quit by now, cashed in my shares in the company and sailed off into the sunset." His arm swept in an arc that took in the sumptuous furnishings and open expanse of the expensive town house. "Sometimes I think I'm going to drown in all this responsibility."

"I've told you what you need," Graydon said sincerely.

"Yeah, yeah, I know. But religion isn't for me."

"I'm not talking about religion. I'm talking about a personal relationship with Jesus. Once you have that, all the other stuff falls into place."

Mark perked up. "So you don't have any trouble with tough challenges?"

"I didn't say that. I have as many problems as

the next guy. The difference is I don't have to face them alone anymore." His eyes narrowed. He thrust his hands into the pockets of his slacks and regarded his brother with suspicion. "Okay, get to the point. What is it you want me to do for you?"

"I thought you'd never ask." Mark was grinning in triumph. "The social workers said they think Melissa will get over her obsession if we can provide closure. They suggested I take her to see Stacy and the dogs so she can thank them for finding her."

"And you don't dare do it because you have a jealous wife. You're afraid she wouldn't understand."

"Bingo. That's why you need to do it for me."

Graydon took a deep breath and released it with a noisy whoosh. "I don't know...."

"Hey, you're the one preaching about your faith all the time. I'd think you'd be happy to put it to the test."

There was no way to refuse without negating everything he'd just said to Mark. Either he trusted the Lord to handle things or he didn't. But another meeting with Stacy Lucas? He had enough to do already thanks to his busy career. The last thing he needed was another complication.

Especially one as pretty and intriguing as the woman he'd encountered in the Ozark Mountains.

"Are we there yet?"

Melissa had asked the same question so many

times Graydon had lost count. "Almost."

"That's what you said before." She wrinkled up her little face in a pout. "I don't believe you."

"Okay. We can always turn around and go home if that's what you want."

"No!"

"Then I suggest you settle down and behave yourself. I've never told you a fib and I'm not telling one now." He pointed to the digital clock on the dashboard of the BMW. "See this? When the hour changes to the number two, we should be getting close."

Subdued, she muttered a sullen, "Okay."

"That's better." Determined to distract her, he glanced at the crumpled, white paper bag in her lap. "Why don't you have a piece of the candy we bought."

The child's small fingers closed in tight fists around the opening of the bag. "No. This is for the rescue lady and the dogs. We can't *eat* it!"

"Oh, I see. Sorry."

"It's okay, Uncle Gray. You didn't know." Her voice grew thready. "I wanted to bring her one of my new dolls but Candace wouldn't let me."

"That's because she bought them for you to play with."

"Uh-uh. She put them on a shelf in my room. All I get to do is look at them, 'cause they're so 'spensive."

"Well, I'll see if I can't talk her into letting you play with one or two. Would you like that?"

"I guess so," Melissa said quietly. She brightened, grinned over at him. "I'd rather have a puppy."

Graydon laughed to himself. He'd walked right into that one, hadn't he? The child might be only six but she was already becoming an accomplished negotiator. "Let me guess. I'll bet you want a dog just like the ones Ms. Lucas has."

"Uh-huh."

He was about to caution her to wait awhile before asking Candace or Mark to buy her a puppy, when she squealed and pointed to the clock.

"Look! There's a two!"

"You're absolutely right. Good for you. And we're right on schedule." Peering at the street signs, he found what he was looking for and turned west. The meandering, narrow road led him farther and farther from town. Small farmsteads and older houses with tree-shaded yards were scattered across the rolling hills. Rural mailboxes indicated their ownership but half of those were unreadable.

Thinking he must be lost, Graydon was about to turn back and try another road when he spotted a hand-lettered sign that read Dog Training. Even if this wasn't Stacy's place, the folks who lived here might know her.

When he slowed and turned into the driveway, Melissa took off the safety belt he'd insisted she wear and got up on her knees to look out the window.

"Sit down, honey," he warned. "I'm not sure this is the right house."

"It is! It is!" she shouted, pointing. "Look!"

There were at least six, maybe seven, dogs visible in the fenced yard at the side of the house. They were jumping and barking with such fervor Graydon couldn't be certain if any of them were the ones he'd met.

He parked, intending to have a look around before he let the child get out of the car. Missy had other ideas. She scrambled after him, darted past and raced up the steps to the front porch. By the time he caught up with her, she'd jumped up and rung the bell.

Concerned that there might be more dogs inside the house, he scooped up the eager child to protect her in spite of her protests.

"I can do it by myself!" Melissa whined.

"I know you can. And I'll let you. I just want to make sure this is the right place before I put you down."

"No!" Melissa was puckering up for a good cry. When the door opened abruptly, she began to smile instead.

It was all Graydon could do to keep from laughing at the comical expression of shock and dismay on Stacy's face. "We were just in the neighborhood and thought we'd drop in," he said. "I hope we haven't caught you at a bad time."

She recovered her poise and closed her mouth. "Oh, no. I always greet my guests wearing my rubber boots and torn jeans. I wouldn't want anyone to think I was putting on airs."

"Good. Is it safe to let Missy down?"

"Of course. All the dogs are in the kennel, but even if they were loose, it would be fine. I wouldn't keep an animal that wasn't gentle around children."

She crouched to be at the same eye level as the little girl as soon as he lowered her to the porch. "I'm so glad to see you're okay, Missy. I've been thinking about you."

"You have?" Melissa's voice was so faint Graydon could hardly hear what she said. After the tantrum she'd thrown in the car, it was a welcome change of tone.

"I sure have. And I'm glad you came to see me. It always makes me very happy when I find somebody who's lost and bring them home safe and sound, like you. It makes my dogs happy, too."

"I got you a present," Melissa said, holding out the wrinkled bag. "I picked it out myself."

Stacy accepted it as if it were worth millions. "Oh, how sweet. Thank you. Can I give you a hug?"

It was Graydon's turn to be surprised. Missy launched herself at Stacy without a word and threw her arms around her neck so enthusiastically she nearly toppled them both over. This from the child who hadn't let anyone touch her for weeks after she'd been placed in Mark's home!

Graydon bent down, reached for Stacy's elbow, and steadied her. "Easy, Missy. We came to thank Ms. Lucas, not break her neck."

The little girl released her hold. "Okay. Can I see the dogs, now?"

"Sure," Stacy told her. "You go around the house. I'll meet you at the gate in a minute." *If I can find the strength to stand up,* she added to herself. For some reason, her legs felt like she'd just run a five-mile obstacle course. Twice. She let Graydon help her to her feet only because she was certain she'd fall flat on her rear if he let go of her arm.

"You okay?" he asked. "You look kind of pale."

"I'm fine. Probably missed lunch again. What time is it anyway?"

"Around two."

"Well, that explains it. Low blood sugar always makes me a little woozy." Stacy was trying to ignore the fact he was still standing close. Too close. And using up all the oxygen so she couldn't get a decent breath of air. If her feet hadn't refused to obey, she'd have stepped back.

"Why don't you look in the bag?" he suggested, smiling.

She cast him a wary glance. "What's so funny?"

"Nothing. Just remember, I wasn't the one who picked out your present."

Stacy parted the top of the bag and peered inside. Bright-orange, red, yellow and green shapes lay in a semitransparent pile. "Oh, wow! Gummi Bear candies! I haven't had any of these since I was little." Grinning, she popped one into her mouth. "I always thought the red ones were the best."

Her childlike enthusiasm was so contagious Graydon forgot himself and joined in. "No way. They all taste the same."

"Do not."

"Do so."

Stacy held out a green bear. "Here. I'll prove it to you." She popped it into his mouth the moment he opened it to argue, then poked around in the bag searching for a different color.

When she chose another candy and held it up for him, he didn't respond right away, so she said, "Come on. Open up. Incoming bear."

He didn't move. Didn't even flinch.

She raised her gaze to meet his. In place of the sparkle of mischief she'd glimpsed in his dark eyes before, there was now a warning. A solemnity that took her by surprise. It sent a frisson of alarm zinging up her spine.

"No," he said softly, hoarsely.

Stacy blinked. Her quizzical gaze returned to his firm mouth, the stubborn jaw she'd noticed when his beard had shadowed it during Missy's rescue.

Something had changed between them in a heartbeat. But what? The air was charged with tension. With indescribable awareness.

She swallowed hard. Had she and Graydon Payne actually been having *fun* together? Was that why the man had suddenly become so reserved? Or had she somehow caused him to withdraw? It was impossible to tell.

Still, she knew *she* had been enjoying herself in his company. Apparently, the Lord wasn't through convincing her that she needed to forgive what had transpired between them in the past. Too bad He hadn't dealt with her brooding guest in the same manner!

If Graydon's mood had plummeted because of her, it was understandable. A man like him wouldn't want to be caught letting his hair down and enjoying himself with somebody who didn't belong to a country club, buy her clothes at exclusive shops or have her hair and nails done professionally.

There he stood, all proper and perfect as ever in his crisp, tailored shirt and impeccably pressed slacks. He came from a totally different world. A place she had no desire to visit, even temporarily. She was more than content with the life God had given her, and she wasn't going to let some good-looking, overbearing, stuffed shirt come along and steal her joy.

"Fine," Stacy said, shoulders square, chin up. "Be a stuffy sourpuss. I'm going to take my candy and go share it with Missy. At least one of you appreciates the simple pleasures of life.''

Graydon stood very still as he watched her walk away. Was he really stuffy? Or was that just how Stacy viewed him? Not that it mattered what she thought. There was no reason why he should care. And no reason why he should find himself so attracted to her, either. That was what unnerved him the most. For an instant, when she'd fed him the candy and her fingers had innocently grazed his lips, he'd had the idiotic urge to take her in his arms and kiss her senseless. Talk about crazy!

Lost in thought, he mulled over their past. It would have been better for everyone if she hadn't misunderstood his motives when they'd first met, years ago. The disillusioned look on her young face was one he'd never forget. He hadn't wanted to hurt her. He'd simply known she was wrong for Mark and he'd said so, as much for her benefit as for his brother's. Stacy had been naive. Innocent. Shy. The strong-willed Payne family would have swallowed her up and crushed the radiant spirit he'd sensed beneath her unsophisticated demeanor. He ought to know.

Only now she wasn't shy, was she? Maybe she wasn't naive, either, in spite of her supposed sweetness. Either way, he didn't intend to stick around and find out. *No, sir!*

Coming to his senses he stepped off the porch and headed for the yard where the dogs were kept. He'd done his good deed for the day. He'd brought

Missy to see her rescuers. Now, it was time to start home.

Graydon's gut knotted again when he thought of his unsettling reaction to Stacy. Clearly, it was *past* time for him to make a hasty exit. Way past time. The sooner he got himself away from her, the better he'd like it.

He went to find Missy.

Chapter Four

When Stacy got to the back yard she found Missy sticking her small hands through the fence and giggling as all seven dogs jockeyed for position to lick her fingers. The comical sight made her laugh, too.

"Hi! Sorry I took so long." Munching on a yellow Gummi Bear, she unlocked the gate, then paused before opening it. "This candy is delicious. Want some?"

"Sure! Can the dogs have a piece, too? I'll share."

"Let's give them doggy treats instead, shall we? They're better for them."

"Okay." Missy stood close at her heroine's heels, waiting for the chance to enter the yard. "I can do it. I'm not scared."

"All right. But first we have to make them sit and behave, or they'll learn the wrong lessons."

"Like what?"

"Like pushing and shoving to get what they want. They have to learn manners, just like you and I do." Stacy noticed the child's smile fading. "What's the matter?"

"Candace says I'm a—a little bar—bar... something."

"Barbarian?"

"That's it." She looked up at Stacy, her eyes wide, her expression hopeful. "I'm not, am I?"

"Well, *I* certainly don't think so." It was hard to keep her opinion of the Paynes to herself. If it hadn't been for the good of the child, she wouldn't have held back or made excuses for them. "Maybe it's just that Candace hasn't been around kids before. Give her time. She'll get used to having you there."

"I wish..."

Stacy sat down on the lawn and opened her arms to the sad little girl. "Come here."

Missy didn't hesitate to crawl onto her lap.

"I know how it is to wish for something so hard you think you'll burst. But sometimes there's just no way for our wishes to come true, even if they are wonderful."

"My—my daddy died," Missy whispered. She wrapped one arm around Stacy's neck and buried her face against her chest.

Deeply moved, Stacy rocked them both back and forth. "It'll be okay, Missy. It'll be okay."

"No, it won't." Her voice was barely audible.

Tell me what to say, Lord, Stacy prayed silently. *Show me how to help her. Please?*

Folding the woeful little girl in a tight embrace Stacy blinked back bittersweet tears as she fully realized why she'd been chosen to minister to Missy. "I do understand how you feel, honey. My mama and daddy both died in a plane crash when I was ten years old."

Melissa drew a shuddering breath. "They did?"

"Uh-huh. We were all flying home for my birthday. The plane had a bad accident. I was riding in the back seat."

The child paled. "Did you get hurt?"

"My leg was broken. And I was very sad," Stacy said simply. "When I got better, they sent me to live with some people who didn't like me very much."

"What did you do?"

Stacy wondered how to phrase her confession so it wouldn't sound as if she were condoning running away from problems. "I was pretty dumb. I ran away and got lost." She looked down to see what the child's reaction was.

Lifting an eyebrow, Missy pressed her lips into a pout. "I don't believe you."

"Why not?"

"Because that's what I did, too. Grown-ups always make up stories like that to fool kids."

"Well, in my case, it's all true," Stacy told her. "The reason I started working with my dogs is because they sent a wonderful dog to find me when

I ran off and got lost in the mountains. When I grew up I decided I wanted to be able to help other lost people the same way.''

Missy got up and faced her, arms folded across her chest. ''No way.''

''I can prove it,'' Stacy countered. ''Want to see my scar?''

''Is it yucky?''

''Not anymore.''

''Okay.'' Missy cocked her head and bent down as Stacy adjusted the hole in the knee of her jeans to reveal a faded scar on her lower thigh.

''See? That's where my leg was broken.''

''Ooooh! Does it hurt?''

''No. But I'm glad I have it.''

Subdued, the girl asked, ''Why?''

''Because I needed the scar to prove to you that I do understand how you feel about losing your daddy.''

''You do?''

''Yes, I do,'' Stacy said with a smile. She knew Missy probably wasn't the only person she'd be able to identify with, to help, because of her injury. But she trusted God to show her more of His marvelous plans as she went along. Right now, it was enough that she believed she'd been led to this particular child at this precise time. ''And I'll try to help you all I can, because that's my job.'' Her grin widened. ''Besides, I like you. You've got spunk.''

''What's that?''

Stacy got to her feet, dusted off her jeans, and stuffed the small bag of candy into her pocket. "It means you're brave. You ask questions. You also have the brains to sort out the answers you get." She tousled Missy's hair. "Come on. Let's go get the dogs their treats."

"I like ice cream. Got any?"

Laughing, Stacy led the way into the yard while the dogs gathered to welcome their master and her diminutive visitor with wagging tails and excited wiggles. "We can look in the freezer and see. You'll have to ask your uncle if you can have some, though."

"Oh, he always lets me have anything I want," Missy said with obvious pride. "He likes me, too."

Stacy heard Graydon calling to Missy and answered for her. "We're back here on the porch. The gate's unlocked."

He came around the corner of the house, paused at the fence and eyed the barking horde. "You sure it's okay?"

"I'm positive. The dogs have been fed recently. Besides, they don't like their dinner on the hoof."

"How comforting."

Stacy laughed at his sardonic expression. "What's the matter? Don't you trust me?"

"Not a whole lot." He opened the gate and stepped through.

"Well, at least you're honest about it." She

waved her licked-clean ice cream stick in the air.
"Wanna join us?"

"No, thanks. We have to be getting back."

Missy began to lean against her.

"You can't go yet," Stacy said. "I promised
Missy I'd put my dogs through their paces before
you left. She wants to see how I train them."

"Maybe some other time."

She knew better than to argue with someone as
stubborn as Graydon Payne so she tried a more
roundabout approach. "Nonsense. It'll only take a
few minutes. A promise is a promise. I make it a
rule to never break mine." She eyed Missy and
added, "Especially where kids are concerned."

Stalling while he decided what to do, Graydon
checked his watch. "All right. I'll give you fifteen
minutes."

"Thirty."

"Twenty," he growled.

"Twenty-five?"

"Don't push it."

"Okay, okay. But I can't show you everything
in a few minutes. You'll have to come back and
visit again." She flashed a hopeful smile in
Missy's direction. The child looked close to tears.
She'd stopped eating her ice cream bar when her
uncle had announced that they were leaving. The
melted sweet was running down her arm. Lewis
was seated by her side, gently licking it off her
elbow before it could drip onto the porch.

"I won't promise that," Graydon said flatly. "I don't make promises I can't keep, either."

"Fair enough." She smiled down at the little girl. "Missy, you wait here and finish your ice cream. I'll be right back." The child simply nodded. It broke Stacy's heart to see her so unhappy.

Focusing on the stubborn man who'd spoiled the lighthearted spirit of the visit, Stacy gestured toward an open field. It stood separate from the kennel and enclosed yard where she exercised her dogs-in-training. "If you'd care to help me, Mr. Payne, we can have a short course set up in a few minutes."

He couldn't think of a polite reason to refuse. The sooner she got her demonstration under way, the sooner he'd be out of there, which sounded good to him.

With a deep sigh, he followed, carefully shutting the gate behind him so the dogs wouldn't get out, then rolling up his shirtsleeves. "Okay. What do you want me to do?"

"I'll need those boxes over there." Stacy pointed. "And the cart with the wooden dumbbells and gloves in it. While you're at it, slip one of them on, will you?"

"Put the gloves on?"

"That's right. One's enough. Just keep it on till I tell you to take it off."

Graydon did as he was told, fascinated in spite of himself. The gloves were old and dusty, as if they'd been around for years. If Stacy's dogs could tell which one he'd worn, with all the other scents that must already be on the worn fabric, he'd be thoroughly impressed.

He used his gloved hand to pull the cart, intending to obscure his scent and make the test as difficult as possible.

"Watch where you walk," Stacy cautioned, leading the way. "Stay on the paths. I haven't mowed this field lately so there are probably a few ticks and chiggers lurking in the long grass."

"Terrific."

"I thought you'd like it." She giggled again.

"Is that why you asked me to help you?"

"No." She lowered her voice. "I wanted a chance to talk to you…alone." Glancing back at the porch she decided they were far enough away to converse without being overheard. "Missy told me her daddy died. What about her mother? Where's she?"

"Died in childbirth," he answered softly. "Her father raised her by himself."

"Which explains why they were so close. What about other family? Relatives? Surely there's someone who can take her in."

Graydon stiffened. "Meaning Mark and Candace aren't fit parents?"

Stacy felt like clobbering him. Instead, she did the Christian thing and faced him squarely, hands on her hips. "No, Mr. Payne. Meaning a child feels lost enough when a parent dies. I was hoping there might be somebody else Missy already knows who could at least befriend her long enough to convince her she's not all alone in the world.''

With a deep sigh he shook his head. "There's nobody.'' The glistening of tears in Stacy's eyes surprised him. "What makes you care so much?''

"Never mind,'' Stacy said. She wiped her eyes, blinked rapidly and changed the subject. "Boy, the sun is sure bright today. Really makes my eyes water. Guess I should have worn my sunglasses.''

"Guess so.'' Graydon wasn't fooled. Stacy Lucas had a giant soft spot in her heart for Melissa the same way he did. It was funny how things worked out. If he hadn't talked her out of marrying Mark, she probably wouldn't have been there to save Missy.

The portent of that thought shook him to the core. What an amazing concept! Even before he'd known he was going to become a Christian, the Lord might have been using him for ultimate good!

That revelation was the most welcome one he'd had for a long time.

"Okay,'' Stacy said, straightening. "The decoys are in place. Give me the glove and go hide behind one of those trees while I go get Missy and one of my dogs.''

He raised an eyebrow. "Over there? Through the grass? I'm already beginning to itch.''

"I could let you borrow Clark's flea-and-tick collar, if he was wearing one. Unfortunately, I use a once-a-month systemic these days. Sorry.''

"I'll bet you are." He heard her stifled laugh as she turned away. She was enjoying his discomfort altogether too much to suit him. "What do I do then, count to ten?"

"Just hide and hold still," she called over her shoulder. "I'll do the rest." She paused to flash him a mischievous smile. "And don't scratch."

"Very funny."

"I thought so," Stacy said. "Be back in a jiffy."

Graydon watched her walk away. There was a simple, unaffected charm about her. Maybe she'd had that kind of appeal all along but he doubted it. Surely he would have noticed. Except that he was an honorable man and she'd been his brother's girlfriend when they'd first met.

He stayed on the paths as long as he could, then waded through the knee-high grass to the nearest good-size tree. A spiderweb brushed his cheek. Gnats buzzed around his head. He didn't even want to think about what might be creeping up his leg under his slacks!

How did he get himself into this mess? Why had he let that woman talk him into becoming a decoy for a pack of addle-brained, four-legged flea-farms? He must be nuts.

Something tickled his leg. Bending over, he rolled up his pantleg to look. There was nothing visible.

"I'm probably imagining things because of all her stupid suggestions about bugs," he grumbled, deciding Stacy had planted the ideas in his mind just to needle him. As soon as he could convince Melissa their visit was over, he was going to get in his car and—

Someone was shouting in the distance but he couldn't make out what was being said. The performance must have started. He hunkered down behind the tree, held very still and waited to be found.

Stacy was worried. She'd arrived back at the house to find that Missy had pulled another disappearing act. Snapping a lead on Lewis's collar she led him from the yard. When she'd promised a demonstration of tracking skills, she'd intended to use Clark or one of the other dogs. Now, however, she needed her best worker.

Anxious to locate the naughty child before Graydon found out and blew his stack, she called out again. "Missy! Missy, where are you?" There was no answering shout. Not even a whimper.

She leaned over Lewis. "Okay, old boy. You must have seen which way she went. Let's go find her."

The dog strained at the leash. Stacy let him take the lead. He started up the path she and Graydon had taken, then veered off into the field. Grass was bent and broken in a zigzag trail anyone could have followed, even without a dog's help. Missy had obviously run randomly. Experience told Stacy that as long as the child stuck to the open field and didn't flee into the woods, everything would be all right.

She called again and again, "Missy? Missy, you get over here. This isn't funny."

Oh, Graydon is going to be so mad, she thought, worried first about the little girl, then about his reaction to her own insistence they stay to see her work her dogs.

"You'd better find her fast, Lewis, or we're all going to be listening to a tirade," she told the eager dog. "I don't know about you, but personally I'd just as soon skip the lecture."

Lewis lunged sideways suddenly. Stacy's boot caught. She missed her footing, tripped and fell. The leash jerked from her hand at the same time the air was knocked out of her lungs. By the time she recovered and rose to her knees, Lewis was out of sight in the long, green, pasture grass.

That's a fine predicament. "Well, Lord, it's all up to you, now," she prayed, realizing she should have asked for divine help long ago rather than rely solely on herself. It was a bad habit she had. Instead of turning a problem over to God the moment it began, she usually waited until things had gotten out of hand, *then* pleaded for deliverance.

"Maybe someday I'll learn." Stacy got to her feet and brushed herself off. "Please, Lord, don't give up on me. I really need your help with this one. That poor kid is a mixed-up mess. I don't know why she ran off this time but I'll bet it wasn't just to cause trouble."

A serene feeling descended slowly upon her, like sunshine melting ice cream or warm oil being poured over her in a blessed anointing. She raised her hands, palms up, and closed her eyes for a moment, wordlessly praising God for being with her, for accepting her, faults and all.

Then she started off after Lewis and the unhappy child.

Peeking from behind his tree, Graydon had seen Stacy leave the yard. He could tell, from the way the dog was dragging her along, that it was definitely not headed for him. Hah! So much for a convincing demonstration of its search-and-rescue skills.

He scowled when he saw her raise a cupped hand to her mouth. What was she doing? Calling him? Why? Was the test over already? Had the dog failed? It must have. It certainly hadn't come close to locating him.

Stepping into the open he shaded his eyes with his hand and squinted into the distance. A light breeze carried Stacy's voice but he couldn't quite make out what she was shouting. Then she seemed to disappear from sight! What in the world was going on?

He'd started back toward the house when she popped up again. Hesitating, he listened carefully. She was calling...*Missy!* Throwing all caution aside he broke into a run, heading straight for Stacy.

She gritted her teeth when she saw him coming. *Oh, dear.* Now there was going to be trouble! Resigned to facing it squarely, she waited the few seconds it took him to reach her.

Breathing hard, Graydon halted right in front of her. "What happened?"

"I don't know. I got back to the house and Missy had disappeared."

"How could she have? There's a yard full of dogs to watch her."

"Don't yell at me," Stacy warned.

"I'm not yelling."

"Oh, yeah?"

He took a ragged, settling breath. "Well, maybe I was. A little."

"That's better. Now calm down and let me tell you what happened. I checked inside the house first. Missy wasn't there. Lewis kept looking in this direction so I brought him out here to find her."

"Well? Where is he?"

Pointing to a swath of bent grass, Stacy said, "He went thataway."

"Without you?"

"I tripped. I could have called him back but I felt Missy would be safer if I just let him go ahead and find her, then followed him."

"Well, why are we standing here talking?" Graydon was still scowling, his anger evident.

"Because Missy is in no immediate danger and I needed to explain the situation to an irate, uncontrolled guy," she said flatly. "Are you going to cooperate or do you need a longer cooling-off period?''

"I'm perfectly calm," he insisted. "Let's go."

"Whoa. Hold it." Stacy grabbed his arm to halt his abrupt departure. "I go first. I've had training in man tracking, too. Lewis and Missy shouldn't be too hard to find as long as you don't go charging off into the grass fouling the clear trail they left. Got that?"

"I've got it," he said, clenching his jaw and staring down at her hand on his arm. He raised his gaze to meet and challenge hers. "Are you through?"

Staring into his dark eyes, she felt his muscles flex beneath her fingers. That combination of visual and physical stimuli created an acute awareness of his masculinity. What was the matter with her? She didn't even *like* this man. Stacy sighed. That was the key. He was a man. And she was a woman. God had created the differences in them as well as the natural attraction. But that didn't mean He expected them to act on every irrational impulse!

She realized she was still touching Graydon. She jerked her hand away. Mere seconds had passed, yet it seemed as if they had stood staring into each other's eyes for hours. She blinked rapidly, ready to defend her actions. To her surprise—and chagrin—the attractive man seemed as awed by the moment as she was. That would never do!

Forcing herself to concentrate on matters at hand, Stacy shook off her befuddlement and led the way into the field, tracking Lewis. Graydon was right behind her.

Chapter Five

Lewis's excited bark echoed from the edge of the forest, leading them directly to Missy. Graydon raced ahead and got there first in spite of Stacy's warning to let her take the lead. He found the dog licking tears off the child's cheeks.

Shoving Lewis out of the way, he fell to his knees and took the six-year-old in his arms. "Oh, honey. Why did you run away? I was so worried!"

She began to sob against his shoulder.

"Don't ever, ever do that again," he said, his voice breaking.

Stacy arrived in time to hear the pathos in his tone. Too out of breath to speak, she rubbed Missy's back to soothe her while Graydon held her tight.

By the time he got to his feet, still carrying the child, Stacy had also recovered. Smiling, she praised Lewis, picked up the leash and spoke to her companions. "Well, now that we know all's well, I suggest we head back to the house and have some lemonade."

"We have to be going," Graydon said, sounding nearly normal in spite of the frigid glare he was bestowing solely upon his hostess.

Obviously, he didn't think much of her offer of hospitality, Stacy mused. Thank goodness Missy was still hiding her face against his neck and couldn't see his expression.

"Well, maybe another time," Stacy said lightly. Waiting for the contradiction she knew he'd offer, she stopped him with a stern shake of her head and a nod toward the shuddering child. To his credit, he understood.

"Maybe," he finally said.

"Good." Stacy kept her voice cordial. "It's always nice to have friends visit. Especially ones like Missy."

She ignored the man's obvious disdain and kept talking as he turned his back and started for the house. "Next time, though, I'd like her to go with me to see my dogs work instead of helping by being the one they're looking for."

The child opened one eye and peeked out at her, showing surprise that a grown-up hadn't figured out that she'd actually been running away again.

Stacy smiled knowingly, then lifted her index finger to her lips in the universal signal for secrecy.

Missy's wan smile in return was all the reward she needed.

They fell into step on the trail, Graydon leading, Stacy following, and Missy grinning over his shoulder at her new friend and confidante.

Stacy's private line rang that evening just as she was finishing dinner. Expecting the caller to be the telemarketer who'd interrupted her at the same time of day for several days running, she answered with a terse, "I told you. I don't buy anything over the phone."

"Neither do I," a deep, masculine voice said.

"Oops." Stacy regrouped. "Wrong person."

"Evidently. This is Graydon Payne."

As if she hadn't figured that out by now. The vibration of his voice had her tingling like a thousand feathers were being brushed across every nerve in her body!

She abruptly sat down to keep from tottering and reverted to a businesslike persona. "How can I help you, Mr. Payne?"

"You can start by telling me just what you thought you were doing by pretending that Missy wasn't purposely hiding from us today."

"Ah. That." Stacy sank back in the chair. "It just seemed the right thing to do, under the circumstances. The poor kid was already miserable. I didn't see any reason to berate her."

"They call that teaching right from wrong," he said sarcastically.

"Except that Missy already knew she'd done wrong. Yelling at her for it wasn't going to make her feel any worse."

"It might have kept her from pulling a stunt like that again," he countered. "Or hadn't you thought of that?"

"Oh, I had, all right. But I know from experience that a lonely, frightened child isn't rational. I don't suppose you took the time to ask her why she ran away from us?"

When he didn't answer immediately, Stacy continued. "I'll tell you why *I* think she did it. She didn't want to leave me and the dogs and go home. Mark and Candace's house may be wonderful—I hope it is—but if it's not the kind of place where Melissa grew up, nothing we say or do is going to make her feel instantly right about living there. Adjustment takes time. And patience."

"Are you through?"

"Unless you want to hear more," Stacy said with a sigh. "Look, Mr. Payne. I've been in Missy's shoes. I know what it's like to be torn from everyone and everything familiar and plunked down in a place where the adults are either too strict because they don't know what else to do, or too lax because they want to be your best buddy. Neither approach works. Missy needs a loving, self-assured parent. Not a jailer. And not a peer in an adult body."

Graydon cleared his throat. "You were orphaned?"

"Yes. I thought you knew."

"No. Mark never mentioned it."

"Probably because he didn't think anyone in your family would care," she said flatly. "I was brought up in foster homes from the age of ten on."

"Did you ever run away?"

Chuckling, Stacy nodded, even though he couldn't see her doing it. "Oh, boy, did I!"

"Why?"

"What difference does it make?"

"To you and me, none. To Missy, maybe a lot. I want to understand where she's coming from, what's making her so skittish." He paused, waited. Finally he said, "Please?"

For some reason it was harder for Stacy to confide in him than it had been to bare her soul to the six-year-old. "I don't know where to start."

"At the beginning would be good."

She imagined she heard a trace of wry humor in his voice and it stopped her. "This isn't funny."

"I never said it was. Look. I know Missy's gotten attached to me but I don't know what to do about it. I have to go to Saint Louis next week on business and I don't want to leave without at least trying to help her cope."

"Will you be gone long?"

"I'm not sure. Why?"

"Because even if you explain the reason for the trip to her, she's going to think you're not coming back, just like her daddy. Especially if you're vague about your plans. If you give her definite information and then stick to it, she'll find the whole concept easier to accept.''

''That's a good idea. Thanks.''

''You're welcome. The other thing you might do is telephone her at a prearranged time each day. It's the uncertainty that's the hardest. Kids live in the present. They have short attention spans and little patience. You and I can look ahead, be willing to wait for what we want. Missy's lost every routine she used to rely on for stability. She needs new anchors, new daily habits to give her a sense of being able to predict a calm, happy future. Provide that and I think you'll see a big change in her.''

''I don't know what to say. I'd never looked at it quite that way. From her viewpoint, I mean. I knew she had to be scared coming to a new home, but I figured the best thing to do was to entertain her, try to distract her. I never dreamed she'd welcome a dull routine.''

Impressed by his candor, Stacy decided it wouldn't hurt to reveal one painful detail of her past she'd always kept secret, even from Mark. ''The other thing to watch out for is too much involvement with the law.''

''In what way?''

She cleared her throat. ''Remember how I said I'd run away? Well, I was habitual. I remember being so angry all the time that I couldn't think straight…and I was a lot older than Missy. I should have figured out how my behavior was hurting my chances of permanent adoption. But I didn't.''

"What happened?" Graydon asked, his voice husky.

"I was locked up for a while when I was in my teens. For my own good, they said." She heard his sharp intake of breath. "That's one reason why I didn't want to make too much out of Missy's vanishing act today. If she gets a reputation as a runaway, the powers-that-be might rescind their recommendation that she be adopted. Please, don't let that happen, Gray." She caught her slip of the tongue. "I mean Graydon…Mr. Payne."

Few besides his brother had ever dared shorten his name. Coming from Stacy as part of a heartfelt plea for Missy's future welfare, however, it seemed appropriate. "You can call me Gray," he said, hoping to sound reassuring. "I won't let anything bad happen to her, Stacy. I promise."

She blinked back tears of relief. "You don't know how glad I am to hear you say that."

The next two weeks passed in a blur. Stacy found herself thinking of Gray and of Missy; most often of Gray. Disgusted with her wandering mind, she buried herself in so much extra work she was exhausted.

If Onyx's puppies hadn't arrived ahead of schedule she'd have thrown herself into bed that night and caught up on her sleep. As it was, she'd spent the hours between midnight and ten the next morning in the whelping shed. The result was seven healthy pups, four of which looked just like Lewis, golden coat and all. The other three leaned more toward the Labrador retriever side of the family tree.

As soon as mother and babies were settled and she was sure there were no more pups coming, Stacy showered, washed her hair, and plopped down on her bed, too weary to even turn back the covers.

The ringing of the telephone roused her. "Ummm. Hello?" she managed. If it was that pesky salesman again, she just might say something very un-Christian.

"Stacy Lucas?" The unfamiliar female voice on the other end of the line sounded skeptical.

Stacy blinked to try to clear her head. Sunlight was streaming through the bedroom window. Either she'd slept more than twenty-four hours or less than three. Since her hair was still damp from shampooing, she assumed it was the latter.

"Is that you, Ms. Lucas? Hello?" the caller pressed.

In no mood for conversation, she yawned. "Yes. I'm sorry. Unless this is an emergency I'd appreciate it if you'd call back. I've been up all night and I'm beat."

The woman's tone became even more formal. "I'm sorry to bother you, Ms. Lucas. This is Mr. Graydon Payne's executive assistant. He asked me to call you. It seems there's a problem at the Payne estate.''

She sat bolt upright and gripped the receiver tightly with one hand while she pushed her damp hair out of her eyes with the other. "What is it? Missy?''

"The little orphan girl? Yes," the woman said. "Mr. Payne says they can't seem to locate her. He was hoping you'd be free to assist them. You'll be well paid for your services, of course.''

Stacy rolled her eyes. Didn't that family ever think about anything besides money? She grabbed a pencil and pad from the nightstand. "Okay. Tell me where the child was last seen.''

"It's my understanding she was visiting at the senior Payne estate, on Lake Norfork, outside of Mountain Home. Are you familiar with the location?''

Stacy pressed her lips into a thin line. Unfortunately, she was well acquainted with the luxurious mansion and grounds. Mark had taken her there several times, trying to impress her. All he'd succeeded in doing was making her feel totally out of place.

"I know where it is," she said. "What else?''

"There's nothing else to tell. When Mr. Payne instructed me to hire you to find the child, he said you'd take care of the details.''

That figured. "All right. Tell him I'm on my way.''

"And your fee?''

Words Stacy hadn't used since her rebellious teenage years bubbled to the surface of her consciousness. She refused to give in, voice them, and disappoint her Heavenly Father. "Six million, give or take a mil," she retorted. "Tell him I'll take it out in Gummi Bears."

Rather than go all the way up to Ash Flat, Stacy cut across on Highways 58 and 69 to Melbourne, then dropped down to Calico Rock on the White River and picked up Highway 5. None of the roads were easy driving. The only good thing was that it was bright daylight. Closer to dusk, she'd have had to slow way down to be ready to dodge whitetail deer crossing the roads.

By the time Stacy started across the four-lane bridge at the south end of Lake Norfork she could feel the tightness in her arm muscles from fighting the old truck on the twisting mountain roads. Her palms were sweaty. Her back was tied in knots of tension. And, like it or not, the closer she got to Mountain Home, the more uptight she was.

She hadn't taken the time to load Lewis's traveling crate in the back of her pickup truck, so he was perched on the seat next to her, panting.

"Yeah, I'm too warm, too," she muttered. "But that's just because I'm rushed. What's your excuse?"

Lewis seemed to smile back at her.

Rolling down the driver's side window, she felt the wind caress her cheek, lifting wisps of her hair.

She glanced down at herself. She'd managed to find a clean pair of nice jeans and a blouse to match, but she hadn't taken the time to fix her damp, flyaway hair or put on any makeup, either.

Oh, well. Who cares? she thought. Instantly, her mind conjured up images of the stiff, conservative Payne family. They'd care how she was dressed even if she were only stopping by to pick up their trash!

Stacy chuckled. "We're going to be about as welcome as a skunk at a Sunday School picnic," she told the dog. "Only this time, I don't care what they think of me."

Fully attentive, Lewis licked his nose, his expressive, chocolate-colored eyes watching her every movement.

She reached over and patted him. "That's what I like about you, kiddo. You're easygoing, friendly, loyal, smart and you never give me any trouble." Unlike the man she was on her way to help, she added.

The silly comparison made her chuckle. "Know what? If Graydon Payne was a dog I'd sell him to the lowest bidder and get a good one like you in his place." She ruffled Lewis's ears as he stretched out on the seat beside her.

Contemplating the classified ad she'd place, her high humor intensified. "I can see it now. 'Good-looking but unteachable man for sale. Will trade for decent dog.'"

That did it. Stacy began to laugh hysterically.

Tears of uncontrolled hilarity filled her eyes and ran down her cheeks. Rather than chance a wreck, she pulled onto the shoulder at the far end of the bridge to wait until she could catch her breath and regain the necessary faculties to continue safely.

Gasping, she wiped her eyes then blew her nose. This was ridiculous. She was tired, yes, but not tired enough to trigger such an absurd reaction. Thoughts of Gray, however, had apparently pushed her over the limits of her ability to cope with the present crisis. Proud of her normal resilience in tense situations, she was astonished to have experienced such a loss of self-control. Thank God it was only temporary!

With a jolt of conscience, Stacy realized thanking the Lord was *exactly* what she needed to do. And had failed to do, as usual.

"Oh, Father, here I go again," she whispered. "I'm sorry. Thank you for putting up with me and for allowing me to help Missy. And thank you for keeping me safe just now when my foolishness could have caused an accident."

A brief memory of the crash that had taken her parents' lives flashed into her mind. "I don't know why things happen the way they do," she prayed. "I only know I believe in You. Please, help me to pass on that kind of trust and peace to that poor, scared little girl."

She sighed. There was more that needed saying, needed turning over to the Lord. Her attitude in regard to the Payne family, for instance. Only she wasn't ready to do that.

Not yet.

Maybe not ever.

The exclusive neighborhood of the Payne estate wasn't particularly intimidating until you drove off the main highway and into the midst of it. The immense houses all had perfectly manicured lawns, well-placed, specimen trees and lots of flowers. Even the outbuildings were larger than the average home.

Temporarily awed, Stacy wondered if she'd be able to distinguish the Payne house from all the others, even if she did manage to find the right street. But she needn't have worried. The moment she glimpsed the mansion her stomach tied in a knot of recognition.

Slowing, she turned into the long, sweeping driveway. It felt odd to be returning to this place under such different circumstances. The last time she'd been there she'd been insecure, eager to impress Mark's parents and totally inept at doing so.

She smiled to herself. *How times change.* And how she'd changed since then! What a blessing!

"Thank you, Jesus," she breathed softly. "I don't know what you have in mind this time, but thanks to You, I'm up to it."

Stacy pulled to a stop in front of the carved stone steps. They led up to a full-length porch supported by fluted white pillars. The whole facade was reminiscent of Southern plantation houses. Except this one looked larger and more elaborate.

"Well, Lewis," she said. "This is it. You ready?"

In answer, the dog thumped his golden tail against the truck seat, making her smile and reach for the door handle. "Yeah, me too. Let's get this over with so we can go back to where the down-to-earth people live."

He woofed, clearly eager to begin. Stacy snapped a leash on his collar and led him toward the front door. Before she could climb the porch steps, Graydon jogged around the corner of the west wing. All in white, he looked as if he'd just stepped off the tennis court.

He waved and called to her. "Over here! Glad you could make it."

Stacy's first reaction was to be relieved she wouldn't have to go inside in order to meet anyone else. Then it occurred to her that he was probably avoiding introducing her to his parents. Particularly his imperious mother.

Nonetheless, she managed a smile as he trotted up. "Hi. I understand you need me again."

"Missy's done another disappearing act." He halted a few feet away when Lewis growled. "I don't suppose you could have brought the one that doesn't hate my guts, could you?"

"Lewis is the best. Besides, I didn't think you still lived here."

"I don't. I have a condo in Searcy. And a little

place on the west shore of the lake, too." He eyed Lewis with caution. "So where do you want to start looking for Missy?"

"You should know the drill by now. We'll need an article of clothing or an object she's touched recently."

Gray reached into the pocket of his white tennis shorts. "Will this do?"

It was a small, bead-filled frog. "It should. Was she playing with it recently?"

"Even slept with it," he said, his expression clearly showing his concern.

"I'll bet you gave it to her. Right?"

"Yes. How'd you know?"

"I assumed as much, judging by her past choices." Stacy took the stuffed toy and held it for Lewis to sniff while she asked, "Where was she last seen?"

"Inside. But mother's had the staff search the house already. I'm not as worried as I'd be if Missy were lost in the woods again, but I didn't know where else to look. That's why I called you."

"You mean you had your executive assistant call me, don't you?" Stacy couldn't help the rancor that crept into her voice.

"That's the same thing."

"Hardly." she said flatly. "I'd been up all night. When the phone rang and woke me, I didn't recognize her voice so I figured she was probably selling something. I almost hung up on her."

Gray lifted an eyebrow and regarded her with curiosity. "And you wouldn't have hung up if it had been me?"

"I didn't say that."

"No, but you insinuated it. What were you doing up all night? Have a hot date?"

"Not that it's any of your business, but I was having puppies."

He cast her a lopsided grin. "My, my. Did it hurt?"

Stacy glowered at him. "Very funny."

"I thought it was. Where's your sense of humor?"

She recalled the experience of near hysteria she'd had on her way there. "I gave it up this side of Norfork. Shall we get down to business? We have a lost child to find."

Chapter Six

Stacy let Lewis take the lead while she guided him in ever wider circles around the perimeter of the Payne house. She'd tried to convince Graydon to let her work alone, to no avail. He was sticking close the same way her dogs guarded a favorite chew toy.

That analogy made Stacy smile in spite of herself. Unfortunately, he noticed.

"What's so funny?" he asked.

"Oh, nothing. You wouldn't understand."

"Try me."

"Not a chance."

He snorted with derision. "I take it your flash of good humor was sarcasm at the expense of my family, then?"

Amazed at how close he'd come to her earlier thoughts, Stacy whipped around to look up at him.

The appealing sparkle in his dark eyes sent a shiver zinging up her spine and made the hair on the nape of her neck tingle. Rather than lie, she decided to refrain from offering any rebuttal.

Gray nodded. "I figured as much. Know what? You have a real problem, lady."

"I beg your pardon?"

"You're a snob."

"I'm a *what?*" She couldn't believe he was serious.

"A snob," he said, accentuating the words. "You think that just because you grew up with less than I did and became a success in spite of your rough childhood, you're somehow better than the rest of us."

"I do not."

"Oh? You could have fooled me."

"I…" Stacy's conscience refused to let her continue the denial. Warmth flowed up to color her cheeks. Surely he couldn't be right about her. Or could he?

"See? I knew it."

"Oh, stop looking so smug," she told him. "I had no idea I was doing that…assuming I actually was."

"You were. Admit it."

She pulled a face. "Okay. Maybe I was. So I'm not a saint yet. But the Lord's working on me. Give Him time." It galled her to admit that God might use a man like Graydon Payne to point out her faults.

"Gladly. As long as you'll give me the benefit of the same treatment. Remember, I can't help how I grew up any more than you can. Or any more than Missy can. All we can do is take each day God gives us and try to do our best with what we have."

"Or don't have," Stacy added. "You're right. I apologize for letting my personal feelings interfere with my work." Looking down at her dog she shook her head slowly. "Speaking of which… Lewis hasn't found any kind of a trail and we've been at it for nearly half an hour. I think we're wasting our time out here."

"If you say so. What now?"

She glanced toward the house. "You need to search inside again."

"Okay. Come on."

Stacy held up her hand, palm out, and began to back away. "Oh, no. Not me. That's where I draw the line."

"Why?" Gray was beginning to regard her knowingly, his head cocked to one side. "You scared?"

"No. I just make it a point to avoid places where I'm not welcome."

"Even when a child needs you?"

"That was a low blow," she said, scowling. "You and I both know Missy's in no danger while she's in the house."

"Assuming that's really where she is," he countered. "What if we've missed something and she's not in there either? What if—"

"Okay, okay." Stacy waved her hand back and forth to stop him. "I get the picture. I'll come with you."

"Into the lions' den?" Gray teased.

"Sure. Why not? If Daniel could do it with real lions, I'm sure I can face your parents one more time." She heard him chuckle quietly. "Just stop acting like you're going to enjoy putting me through this. Okay?"

"Not a chance," he said. "If I wasn't so worried about Missy, I'd probably sell tickets to all my friends. My parents would have eaten you up and spit out the pieces if I hadn't interceded the last time you were here. But they don't have a clue how much you've matured since then. I can't wait till they find out. It should be quite a show."

The inside of the house hadn't changed much since the last time Stacy'd been there. At least she didn't think it had. With all the antiques and ornate furniture, it was hard to tell. Gray led Lewis and her in via a side door and detoured through the kitchen to explain the circumstances to the cook and butler.

An elderly groundsman, Euless Feeters, was seated at the kitchen table having lunch. He smiled and stood with the rest of the staff when Gray introduced Stacy. "How do, ma'am. Y'all have any luck?"

"None," Stacy said soberly. She addressed the group. "Can any of you think of some special places Missy liked to play around here?" The cook and butler both shook their heads.

So did Euless. He snorted. "Naw. Poor little thing was never allowed out of the house, far's I know. Shame, too. To listen to Nathan, a body'd think it was a blamed sin to enjoy nature." He shot a contrite glance toward the younger Payne. "'Scuse my French."

"No problem," Graydon said. "I agree with you. Besides, you knew Dad when he was a boy. You and Grandpa Nate go way back. Far as I'm concerned, that entitles you to say whatever you want."

"Darn right. Me and ole Nate used to run trot lines up and down the White and jug for catfish when we got hungry." He stared into the distance, obviously remembering, then chuckled. "Course, a fella had to tie up them jugs real good or those big river cats'd take off with 'em, hook, line and all."

Stacy listened, amazed. "You mean, the Paynes weren't always wealthy?"

Feeters cursed colorfully, making Stacy and the cook blush. "Poor as church mice," he went on. "Just like me and mine. Then ole Nate met Anna and wanted to settle down, so he bought some acreage down on the Arkansas, south of here. Came time to sell it and move on, he made a pretty penny, I'll tell you. Invested it all. That's how he got started.''

She glanced up at Graydon. ''Is that true?''

''Sure is. Grandpa was always proud of the way he'd worked his way up in the world.''

''Ought to of stayed right where he was, if you ask me. All that money caused nothin' but trouble when he up and died.'' Feeters glanced down at Lewis. The dog was seated politely at Stacy's side, drooling. ''You fixin' to take that hound into the rest of the house whilst your mama's at home, boy?''

''Of course.'' Gray grinned at the old groundsman. ''Why? You want to watch?''

''Oh, no. Not me.'' Feeters scooped up the remains of his sandwich, grabbed his faded baseball cap and started across the kitchen. ''I know better than to be within a hundred miles a this place when that woman gets a gander at you and that dog in her fancy parlor.'' Laughing and shaking his head, he ducked out the door.

Gray looked at Stacy and gestured toward the archway leading to the main part of the house. ''Shall we?''

Heaving a telling sigh, she complied. ''Okay. But I wish I was going with Mr. Feeters. I think he's the smart one around here.''

''Don't worry. I won't let Mother pick on you the way she used to. Not much, anyway.''

''Very funny.'' She shot a withering glance over her shoulder at him, then remembered what he'd said about her being a snob in reverse. It had helped to hear that the Paynes hadn't always been rich. It made them seem more human. She was curious to know the details. "Tell me about your grandfather's farm."

"The one he sold? There's not much to tell. It was just bottom land along the Arkansas River, like Euless said." He hesitated for effect, then added, "I think they call the place South Little Rock, now."

Gray's parents, Estelle and Nathan Payne, were seated in the drawing room when Graydon ushered Stacy and her dog into their presence. Before either of them could do more than gasp in surprise, Gray said, "We've been all over the grounds. Missy's not there. We're going to check the house."

Nathan jumped to his feet seconds before his wife. "You'll do nothing of the kind! The servants have already done that."

It surprised Stacy to realize she felt briefly threatened. Apparently, she hadn't lost all her youthful dread of encountering the elder Paynes again. At her side, Lewis tensed and growled. Nathan backed down visibly.

"Really, Graydon..." his mother began.

It was the look of disdain in Estelle's eyes that gave Stacy the confidence boost she needed. Stepping forward, Lewis heeling at her side, she smiled pleasantly and extended her free hand. "I guess you don't remember me, Mrs. Payne. I'm Stacy Lucas. I used to be a friend of Mark's.''

"Oh, really?" She made no move to shake Stacy's hand. "How nice."

Amused by the rebuff, Stacy stepped back. "Actually, it was for the best that we stopped seeing each other. I'm glad he's found someone like Candace."

The older woman stared. "You know Mark's wife?"

"Not personally. I saw her at the Spring River Campground with Mark, the first time Missy ran away."

"Oh?" Estelle's eyebrow arched.

Stacy's indignation was rapidly waning, leaving her feeling contrite about the antagonistic thoughts that kept popping into her head. Obviously, the Lord wasn't through showing her that she had a long way to go before she could claim she'd completely forgiven the elder Paynes.

She spoke her conclusions. "Look, I came to find a lost child, that's all. As soon as I find her, I'll be out of your hair for good." A subtle smile lifted the corners of her mouth. "That's a promise."

Nathan found his voice. "Now see here, Graydon…"

Stacy sensed Gray close behind her. To her surprise, Lewis tolerated his nearness this time.

"Well, Dad, we could always call the authorities instead. I'm sure your ritzy neighbors would be thoroughly entertained by a horde of uniformed officers combing this place from one end to the other. It should make quite a show.''

Estelle spoke up. ''That won't be necessary, Graydon. I'm sure you can look after Ms. Lucas for us.''

The implication of mistrust was clear to Stacy. It struck her so funny she temporarily gave in to her all too human urge to tease. She gazed up at her protector and batted her lashes dramatically. An overly sweet smile graced her lips. ''Will you look after me, Gray? Make sure I don't go anywhere I don't belong? Maybe count the silver when I'm done?''

He didn't merely chuckle in response, he roared. She was leaning so close to his broad, strong chest that she could actually feel the vibrations of his hearty laughter.

Her pulse thudded in her temples. Made her dizzy. It took enormous willpower to convince herself she could step away from Gray without falling flat on her face in front of the elder Paynes.

He seemed to sense her need of physical as well as emotional support so he gently cupped her elbow as he said, ''Honey, I'll even frisk you before you leave, if that's what it takes to please everybody.''

Estelle's sharp gasp was barely audible, thanks to the peals of raucous laughter again coming from Graydon as he formally escorted Stacy and Lewis out of the room and closed the door behind them.

* * *

When they reached the hall, he paused to gain control of his sense of humor. His hand remained firmly on Stacy's elbow. "You okay?"

"I'm fine." Her grin was so wide it made her cheeks hurt. "On the way over here, I told Lewis we'd be about as popular as a skunk at a Sunday school picnic. That analogy didn't even begin to describe what just happened."

Gray smiled down at her. "You have to get used to them. They're not as bad as they seem."

"Yeah, right. And I'm the Queen of Sheba."

He bowed low with a flourish. "Your humble servant, your majesty. Where shall we begin the search?"

Stacy was tempted to suggest his parents' suite upstairs, simply to vex them more, but she resisted the urge. "Wherever they let Missy play, I guess. Does she have any toys here? Any place she calls her own?"

"Not really." He sobered. "Mother was supposed to be baby-sitting for Mark and Candace. She's done it before, although she usually hired someone else to come over and do the actual supervision."

"But not this time?"

"I don't think so. That's probably what went wrong. In case you haven't noticed, my mother is not the world's most grandmotherly person."

Stacy rolled her eyes. "No kidding." A rush of sympathy for the little boy Gray had been surprised her. Softly, she said, "It must not have been easy growing up in this house."

"It was okay. Mark fared better than I did." The last vestiges of his smile faded.

"Probably because he was the youngest," she volunteered.

"Probably. It's always hardest on the firstborn."

"I wouldn't know. I was an only child."

"Do you have any family left?" His voice was low, the words compassionately spoken.

"The best anybody could hope for. My family is my church, my Christian friends. I don't know what I'd do without their love and acceptance."

"Plus your dogs," he reminded her.

Stacy laid a hand on Lewis's head, her fingers ruffling the fur behind his silky ears. "That goes without saying. These guys are more than just a job. They're the reason for my existence." She straightened. "So let's get back to work. Take me to the place Missy was last seen and we'll begin there."

Gray led the way to a sweeping staircase framed by carved newel posts and a mahogany banister. In the corner of the bottom step sat a beautiful porcelain doll dressed in pink satin and lace. It had blue eyes and its hair was the same strawberry-blond color as Missy's.

"Mother said she left her playing right here." Gray pointed to the step.

"I'm surprised she didn't take her doll with her." Picking it up, Stacy held it for Lewis to sniff.

His tail began to wag even before she said, "Find."

Making several false starts then changing his mind, the dog finally settled on a path through the sitting room to the atrium. Once there, however, he quickly doubled back.

When he returned to the stairs, Gray said, "Humph. He's as confused as we are."

Stacy wasn't discouraged. She'd seen too many miraculous rescues to doubt her dog's abilities. The problem wasn't Lewis, it was the proper interpretation of his actions. "Not necessarily. Simmer down, stand clear and give him time to sort it all out. Obviously, Missy wandered all over down here, which makes things even harder. He's just looking for the most recent scent trail."

Lewis glanced up at Stacy as if to confirm her statement, wheeled, and took off at a run, pulling her along behind him. He bounded halfway up the staircase, then stopped and began pawing frantically at the carpeting that covered the steps. Little tufts of rose-colored wool drifted downward.

"Oh, terrific," Graydon muttered, swatting at the bits of fuzz like he'd shoo away a fly. "Mother's going to love this." He looked back at the drawing room door to make certain it was still closed the way he'd left it. They'd never find Missy if his mother appeared and demanded that Lewis be banished for digging up her new carpeting.

Stacy was confused, too. She bent over the dog.

"No, Lewis. No. That's impossible. She can't be there."

"No kidding." Gray peered up at them from between the banister posts. The dog was clearly refusing to heed her warning. "Can't you do something with him? He's tearing the place apart."

Stacy pulled Lewis up on a tight leash, sat down on the step he'd been trying to scratch his way through, and smoothed the ragged edge of the carpeting with her hand. The dog seemed to relax. He laid his chin on her lap and looked soulfully up at her.

Thoughtful, she stroked his broad head. There had to be a logical reason for his strange behavior. But what? If Missy had played up and down the steps, leaving a stronger scent trail there than anywhere else, the dog should have taken that route in the first place. Why hadn't he? And why tear at the carpet all of a sudden?

Gray was standing at the landing, shaking his head and talking to himself. Stacy ignored him. So did Lewis. Then the dog startled. His ears pricked. His head cocked. His tail began to thump.

She listened. The muttering man at the foot of the stairs was distracting. "Hush up," she ordered, waving a hand at him. "Listen."

"To what? Your dog tearing up my mother's house? I'll have plenty to listen to when she sees the damage."

"Not that. Lewis hears something. If you weren't making so much noise maybe I could, too." She leaned back and rested her ear on the step above.

At first, all she heard was the thrumming of her own pulse. Then there was a whimper, a sob. *Missy!*

Stacy jumped to her feet. "She *is* here! Is there a closet or something like that under the stairs?"

"Yes! A little storage area that nobody uses." He clapped a hand to his forehead. "Why didn't I think of that? I used to crawl under the table and open the door so I could hide in there when I was a kid."

Circling the arch of the staircase ahead of Stacy and Lewis, Gray shoved aside the heavy library table that hid the small, low door from view. "I doubt even the servants know this is here. The catch is hidden in the paneling so it doesn't spoil the decor. I remember how it works."

He tried twice. "It's stuck."

"Well, do *something*," Stacy said, holding the taut leash. "Lewis can hear her crying and he's going nuts."

Gray grasped the rusty latch and gave a jerk. The door popped open. Missy erupted from the dark little space with a shriek and launched herself straight into his open arms. She was sobbing incoherently.

Stacy stood back and waited while man and child held a heart-rending reunion. *Thank you, Lord,* she prayed silently, letting tears of relief and joy slide freely down her cheeks without embarrassment.

When Gray finally stood and looked at Stacy, his eyes were moist, too. Missy, still drawing ragged breaths and sniffling, hid her face against his shoulder and gripped his neck as if she never intended to let go.

"I don't know how we can thank you," he said hoarsely. "When the door jammed, I guess she couldn't get it open again. If it hadn't been for Lewis..."

"It's all over now. Everything will be fine," Stacy assured him. To her surprise, Estelle bustled past and tried to take Missy from Gray. The child clung to him and refused to budge. When the older woman turned to face her, Stacy could see real grandmotherly concern lurking beneath her cosmopolitan facade.

Behind Stacy, Nathan cleared his throat and said, "Good. Then I assume you'll be going?"

Before she could respond, Gray was at her side, his free arm slipped protectively around her shoulders. "We're all going," he told his father. "I promised Missy an ice cream cone and Ms. Lucas is accompanying us."

Stacy opened her mouth to object, then changed her mind when she saw the raw determination in her champion's expression. At least his ploy would get them all out of the house without further controversy. For that she was grateful. The less time she had to spend in that oppressive house with those people, the better she'd like it.

Gray guided her out onto the porch, then released her and shifted Missy so he could carry her more easily. "I'm so sorry, Stacy. I don't know what's the matter with him. You'd think, after all you've done..."

"It's my job," she said formally. She held out her hand, offering to shake his. "Goodbye, Mr. Payne. I'm glad Lewis and I could be of assistance."

It wasn't clear what happened next, although Stacy did think she saw Missy reach out to her first. In the blink of an eye she was enveloped in a double hug; one from the child, the other from Gray.

Acting solely on instinct she wrapped her arms around them both and rested her forehead against the man's chest. Perfect tranquility enveloped her, flowed through her. For those few seconds, everything in the whole world seemed right. It was a blessed moment she knew she'd never forget as long as she lived.

When Gray loosened his hold and Stacy stepped back, she was surprised to see a sense of pure wonder in his face, in his eyes. Apparently, he'd been as deeply affected by their unexpected mutual embrace as she had.

Chapter Seven

Stacy started to walk away. Gray stopped her with a touch on her arm. "Hey. I thought we were going out for ice cream." Missy was nodding in decisive agreement.

"I have to be going," Stacy insisted.

"Why? You got a hot date?"

Noting the mischievous twinkle in his eyes, she answered, "I'm exhausted from lack of sleep. Puppies. Remember?"

"I *love* puppies," Missy piped up. "Can we go see them?"

"Maybe when they're older," Stacy said. "Right now, they're probably as tired as I am. So is their mommy."

"Is Lewis their mommy?" the little girl asked.

"No, honey. But he is their daddy. Some of them even look like him."

"I looked like my daddy," Missy said sadly.

"Me, too," Stacy told her. "I think that's nice, don't you?"

"I guess." She wrapped both thin arms around Gray's neck and tucked her head onto his shoulder. "Can we go get ice cream, now?"

The imploring look she gave Stacy melted her resolve. "Okay. But only if Lewis can come along. You two lead. We'll follow in my truck."

Gray brightened. "Nonsense. There's no sense in that. We can all go in my car."

"Nope," Stacy said flatly. "Lewis goes or I don't."

"I meant for him to. Come on." He led the way to a shiny black BMW parked under a portico at the corner of the house and opened both passenger doors. "Dogs and kids in the back on account of the air bags."

That left Stacy with only two options. She could share a crowded space with Missy and Lewis, who had already made themselves at home, or she could ride up front with Gray like she would if they were on a date. Her pulse fluttered. Where did *that* idea come from?.

"I'd rather just follow you," she hedged. "It'll be much easier when it comes time for me to head on home."

His gaze was a challenge. "Why? Are you scared of me?"

"Of course not. Why should I be?"

"I didn't say you should. I was just asking a

simple question. It seemed like you were trying to avoid me.''

''Don't be silly.'' Disgusted, Stacy slipped into the front seat. She glanced back, noting that Missy was engrossed in telling Lewis a story. Nevertheless, she spoke softly to keep her negative opinions private. ''Just because your parents hate my guts and my dog dug up your mother's expensive carpeting doesn't mean you and I can't be friends.''

Gray followed her lead with a hoarse whisper. ''Hey, don't forget my brother and his wife. I don't think Mark was too glad to see you again, either. Candace is the jealous type. Keeping her happy makes his life real interesting.''

''Well, she sure shouldn't be jealous of me,'' Stacy said, speaking more naturally. ''She's not only beautiful, she's a sophisticated, poised, high-class lady. Mark's a lucky guy.''

''You didn't say so when you were talking to my mother.''

''Yeah, well… I suppose my pride got in the way. And maybe my old problem with reverse discrimination. If Candace has the confidence to fit into your family, which she apparently does, then I can't help but admire her. She's a lot more flexible and resilient than I'll ever be.''

''She's not prettier,'' he said.

Stacy's mouth dropped open in shock. She snapped it closed and pulled a face. ''Don't be silly. Look at me. I went to bed with wet hair so it's all frizzy, I have no makeup on and my nails are short and chipped from hard work.''

"I'll bet you clean up nicely, though,'' he deduced, adding a wry grin. "I'll have to take you out to dinner sometime so you can show me.''

"In your dreams, mister.'' She'd been staring at his profile while he drove. The funny look he got on his face when she mentioned *dreams* made her stomach flutter. It felt like it came to rest in a big lump, halfway up her throat.

Blushing slightly, he cast her a sidelong glance. "As a matter of fact, I have dreamed about you once or twice.''

"I don't think I want to hear about it.''

"Maybe you should,'' he said soberly. "You see, I dreamed I was apologizing for causing you and my brother to break up.'' When Stacy didn't comment, he continued. "I'd like to do the same thing for real. I'm sorry. I shouldn't have interfered in your lives.''

"No, you shouldn't have,'' she said quietly. "But not for the reasons you think. I told you, you did us both a favor. In retrospect, God's hand in the matter is perfectly clear, even though I couldn't see the truth back then.'' She sighed, rested her head against the back of the leather seat, then continued. "Mark and I were…are…from different worlds. I didn't fit into his world and he'd never have been happy in mine. We'd have made each other miserable trying to become something we weren't, instead of being satisfied with who we really were.''

"And you might not have started working in search and rescue," Gray said. He glanced lovingly at his future niece in the rearview mirror. "Then where would we be?"

"There'd have been someone else willing to step in and help," she said. "I'm just glad I got the chance to meet Missy. She's a sweet little girl. We have a lot in common.''

"I know. She told me more about your past than you did. Which is another reason I should apologize. I had no idea what you'd gone through.''

"That doesn't change a thing," Stacy said wisely. She gestured at the plush leather and wood-grained interior of his luxury sedan. "I don't belong in a car like this anymore than you belong in a beat-up old truck like mine.''

"You shouldn't be ashamed of it.''

"There's no shame involved. Just female logic.''

"That's an oxymoron.''

Stacy squinted over at him. "What is?''

"Female and logic," he said, smiling. "There is no such combination.''

"Oh, yeah? Prove it.''

"I don't have to," Gray said, clearly joking. "All I have to do is listen to you talk and I have no doubt, whatsoever.''

Missy and Lewis had both fallen asleep by the time the party arrived at the ice cream parlor. The dog revived faster than the six-year-old. Groggy, Missy was not the sweet little girl she'd been.

"I wake up like that a lot," Stacy said as she watched Gray trying to rouse the grumpy child. "Too bad we can't give her a cup of coffee. That always helps me."

"If I hadn't promised her a cone I'd let her sleep." He straightened with Missy in his arms. "Think we can get two whole scoops down her while she's napping?"

That did it. Missy rubbed her eyes with closed fists and mumbled, "I want pecan. With sprinkles."

He made a sour face that Stacy found comical. "I know," she agreed. "It sounds awful. But it's her choice."

"What do you and Lewis want?"

"He'll have a single scoop of vanilla, in a dish, and I'll have rocky road, please." She giggled. "He won't need a spoon but I will."

Gray elbowed his way into the shop still carrying the sleepy child. He ordered, then realized he couldn't reach the wallet in his back pocket without putting down Missy and the cones he was already holding. When he tried, the little girl clung to his neck with both arms and whimpered.

"I seem to have a slight problem," he said. "Stacy, would you get my money out for me? It's in my right hip pocket."

"I don't know if I should," she drawled. "The

logical thing for you to do would be to pass me the cones and then get your wallet yourself.'' The incredulous look on his face told her she'd scored a victory. "Of course, I could be wrong. After all, I am just an irrational woman so you might want to rethink the whole problem before you decide." She placed the plastic dishes he'd ordered for her and Lewis back on the counter and held out her hands. "Well?"

Gray handed her the cones. Supporting Missy with one arm, he managed to retrieve his wallet and pay the clerk. As soon as Stacy offered the candy-sprinkled cone to the girl, she wriggled out of her uncle's grasp, grabbed the treat with both hands and forgot all about hanging on to him.

They made their way back outside to where Lewis waited beneath a white wrought-iron table. "As soon as you're finished, Missy, you can hold Lewis's dish for him, okay?" Stacy said.

"Okay." The child chose a chair closest to the dog and licked at her cone so vigorously that she knocked off the top scoop. It rolled onto the table. "Oops."

Gray expected her to cry. Instead she shot him a guilty glance and asked, "Can I give that to Lewis, too?"

"If Stacy says it's okay."

The little girl's pleading, innocent look didn't fool Stacy one bit. She grinned knowingly. "I'll put it in his dish for you. You still have to finish your cone."

"I know. I will," Missy insisted. "I'm almost done."

"So I see," Stacy said. Looking over at Gray, she saw him nod and smile with understanding. She sighed. It seemed strange to be sitting there with him and Missy, eating ice cream and behaving like a real family.

Her eyes widened at the thought. Quickly, she averted her gaze and concentrated on her rapidly melting ice cream. A family? With a Payne? *Never!* Been there, done that…or tried to…and it wasn't fun. Neither was visiting the scene of her youthful rebuff less than an hour ago.

Recalling the confrontation, she chuckled to herself. It had felt good to feel equal to Estelle and Nathan for once. And Euless, the old man she'd met in the kitchen, had been charming. Facing the Paynes had been worth it just to learn the fact that Gray's paternal grandfather had once been dirt-poor. Too bad the more recent generations hadn't benefitted from such a realistic upbringing.

Maybe that was why they went to such lengths to prove they were socially above everybody else; to pretend they were something they really weren't. That notion didn't excuse their behavior but it did put it in a more acceptable perspective. She'd had to do the same kind of thing when her parents were killed. Only with her, the pretense wasn't one of wealth. It was one of happiness and stability.

Stacy recalled all the times, years ago, when

she'd cried herself to sleep because she'd felt so alone. And the times she'd fled from perfectly fine foster homes because they couldn't offer her the permanence she sought. It wasn't until she was nearly grown that she'd finally understood she could never go back, never again be the secure, happy child she'd once been.

She felt a gentle, light touch on her arm and glanced up. Gray was looking at her with concern.

"You okay?" he asked.

Stacy mentally shook herself. "I'm fine. Why?"

"Because you were a million miles away just now. And you looked pretty melancholy. What were you thinking about?"

"The past," she said quietly.

He withdrew his hand and leaned back in his chair. "Ah, that. Would you like to talk about it?"

"Not here. Not now." And not with you, she added to herself. Casting a glance at Missy she changed the subject as she held out the plastic dish. "Okay, honey. You ate all your cone. Now you can give this to Lewis. Just hold on to it so he doesn't push it all over the sidewalk when he tries to lick it."

The little girl looked down, then wailed, "Ugh! He slobbered all over my new shoes."

Stacy stifled a giggle. "That's because he's hungry and he knows you're going to give him a treat. He's a good dog. He's been waiting very patiently while we all ate but he can't help drooling a little."

"That's okay. I can fix him." Missy was matter-of-fact. Taking her napkin, she carefully wiped the dog's chin, talking to him, nose to nose, as she blotted his muzzle. "It's not your fault, Lewis. I'll take care of you."

Amused, Gray watched the child's interaction with the unflappable dog. No wonder Stacy valued him so much. He was more than a rescuer, he was a healer. His presence, alone, had brought Missy out of her shell and enabled her to think of something other than her own loss. He wondered how long it had taken Stacy Lucas to do the same when she was left all alone like Missy.

The sudden urge to take Stacy in his arms and protect her until all the old pain was banished caught him by surprise. Naturally, doing anything like that was out of the question. Still, it did give him a warm feeling to think of repaying her heartfelt kindness with a dose of the same. There was too little love in the world as it was. He didn't like to admit to being such a softy, but he already loved his future niece as if she'd been a part of his family from birth.

Gray smiled to himself and leaned sideways to watch what was going on under the table. Missy was trying to hold the slippery dish still while Lewis's wide tongue sloshed half-melted ice cream over the rim and onto her hands. Instead of complaining about the mess, she was laughing and reassuring the dog that she could give them both a bath if need be. Maybe getting her a puppy was a good idea after all. Of course, if he did such a thing without permission, the rest of the family would threaten to disown him....

His thoughts crystalized. Froze. *Disown him, indeed.* Now there was an interesting memory.

He snorted with contempt. A scene like the one he'd had with his father when he'd turned down the offered junior vice presidency was something he never wanted to experience again. Nathan's angry response, however, had answered a lot of the questions Gray had been afraid to ask. It had also explained why he'd always felt like an outsider, even though he knew of no valid reason for the alienation he sensed at the time.

A gentle touch on his forearm brought his thoughts back to the present.

"Now, it's my turn to ask you," Stacy said. "Want to talk about it?"

Gray tensed, withdrew. "I don't know what you mean."

"Okay. Have it your way. I was just trying to be nice. You looked like you'd just lost your best friend and I thought—"

"It's none of your concern."

"I wish you were right," she said cynically. "But we're both Christians."

He scowled over at her as he got to his feet. "What's that got to do with it?"

"Well, for one thing, we're supposed to be recognizable by the concern and the love we show for one another."

"Where does it say that?"

"I think it's in the thirteenth chapter of John."

"Terrific."

Stacy bristled. "Hey, don't take it personally. I wasn't thrilled when the verse popped into my head, either. Truth to tell, I'm having a terrible time accepting the fact that God expects me to love you as my brother."

A peculiar expression came over him, causing her to study his face, to look deeply into his eyes. If anyone had asked her at that moment, she'd have had to say she was seeing pure anguish. In seconds he'd returned to normal.

"I have enough brothers," Gray said flatly. "And sisters. But thanks, anyway."

Stacy closed her eyes for a moment and sighed. *Father, I'm stuck, again. I don't know why I'm here or what You want me to do. I don't mind helping Missy, but that man is impossible! I can't deal with him. I can't relate to him. I just can't.*

In her heart, in her mind, in her soul, she sensed an unmistakable contradiction. Like it or not, this was where the Lord wanted to use her, at least for the present. She could only hope her tenure was almost up because she was becoming very confused over the jumble Graydon Payne had made of her normally stable emotional state. First she liked him. Then she didn't. Then she felt compassion, instead. Then she remembered what he'd put her through with regard to Mark and the Payne family and she practically loathed him, again. The inconsistency of her feelings was driving her crazy!

Worse yet, the more she was around Gray, the more she noticed how handsome and appealing he was, in spite of her resolve to ignore that aspect of him.

Following him to his car, she watched while he patiently wiped Missy's sticky hands and face, then helped her into the back seat and fastened her safety belt.

Touched, Stacy purposely looked away and focused her thoughts on the sidewalk, on her shoes, on anything but the tenderness he was exhibiting toward the waif. She didn't want to perceive Graydon Payne as a man who would someday make an excellent father. It made her far too aware of her single life, of her choice to remain alone rather than give up her God-given career for anyone's sake. It was a conscious decision. One that she'd prayed about and reaffirmed over and over, positive that her choice was the right one. That decision still stood.

Even divine assurance, however, wasn't enough to keep a shiver of loneliness from skittering up her spine and lodging in her heart.

Chapter Eight

"Do you have any objection to my dropping Missy off at Mark's before we go back to get your truck?"

"No. Why should I?"

"I thought you might be uncomfortable going there, that's all."

Stacy twisted in the seat to partially face him and shook her head slowly, pensively. "You still don't get it, do you? I wouldn't go back and start over with Mark, even if I had the chance. I'm *thrilled* that he's married to Candace because that's just more proof I understood what the Lord had planned for my life."

"You mean your work?"

"Of course." She glanced behind her. Lewis had curled up on the back seat and Missy was using him for a pillow. The picture of the two of them dozing so contentedly was a delight. "Oh, look."

Gray glanced in the mirror. "Uh-huh. Cute. I think we wore them out." He smiled over at Stacy. "You must be beat, too, after being up all night."

"I'd forgotten about that till now. You're right. I am pretty tired."

"Then I'll take you to your truck first. It's not that far out of my way and Missy's asleep anyway. She'll never know the difference." His grin widened. "Until her pillow gets up and goes home with you, that is."

"Lewis is a great dog. That's why I'm using him to sire pups while I can." She sighed happily. "I can imagine his offspring pulling me through the woods till I'm old and gray. If not, I can always fall back on my other training."

"Other training?"

"Yes." Leaning her head back against the seat, Stacy explained. "There's a law enforcement training academy in Tennessee that gives classes in man-tracking. It's a tough course but worth every drop of sweat it takes to pass."

"Sounds fascinating."

Stacy studied his profile as he drove, looking for any sign he was making fun of her. Detecting none, she went on. "It is. It's also the hardest thing I've ever done. They lay a trail but it's booby-trapped, just like it would be if you were following a smart criminal who was determined to stop you any way he could. The test goes on day and night. To pass, you have to find your quarry without tripping one of the traps.''

''Isn't that kind of dangerous?'' His brow was furrowed.

''Not really. We worked in teams. There was a security man following with a radio in case any of us got hurt.''

''Hurt? How?''

''Well, there were hidden pits, water obstacles, planted copperhead snakes, cliffs to rappel down on ropes....''

Gray held up his hand. ''Whoa. I don't think I want to hear any more.''

''Why not? Not your style?''

''Not even close,'' he admitted. ''I like it better when we're following your dogs. At least that way nobody's likely to get hurt.''

''Oh, I don't know. A person could get tangled up in the leash and be dumped on his south end.''

Gray's head snapped around. ''You saw that?''

''Uh-huh. It was quite a show.''

''Thanks,'' he said, making a silly grimace. ''How did you know I wasn't seriously hurt? I might have been.''

''Not a chance. You landed on your brains. Besides, I could hear you yelling at Clark. Such language.''

''I didn't cuss.'' He squinted over at her. ''Did I?''

''No, you didn't. I was just teasing. Actually, I

thought you handled yourself quite well for a novice. Clark's not an easy dog to work with."

"At least he likes me," Gray said, glancing at the sleepers in the back seat. "I wish I could figure out why Lewis took to Missy so easily, yet he won't warm up to me."

"That's probably because of the conflict between us. He's very sensitive to my feelings. Sometimes he knows I'm upset even before I do."

"Are you upset, now?"

Stacy didn't like the brief, penetrating look he gave her. She hesitated. It would have been easy to tell a lie, just a little fib, and be done with their conversation. But it wouldn't have been fair.

"No, I'm not upset," she finally said. "It wasn't much fun facing your folks but the confrontation did have its useful elements. For instance, the way you stood up for me was very nice. I should have told you so sooner. I really appreciated the moral support."

"My pleasure, Ms. Lucas," he said with a grin. "You did a pretty good job yourself."

"I did, didn't I?" Her smile grew to equal his. "The look on your father's face when we walked in together was priceless."

"Did you see Mother's expression? She looked like she'd swallowed a lemon."

"More like an unripe, wild persimmon," Stacy said. "Ever eat one of those? They'll leave your mouth puckered for hours."

"Afraid I haven't had the pleasure," Gray told

her. "If my cook doesn't buy it at the market, I don't eat it. Safer that way."

"But not nearly as much of an adventure," she countered. "You should cut loose once in a while. Enjoy yourself. Act more like your paternal grandfather. I'll bet he was a fascinating person. You must have inherited at least some of his venturesome spirit."

Gray shrugged and sighed. "I wish I could say I had. Nate was quite a guy." He wheeled his car into the drive and sped toward his parents' house, coming to a stop next to the rose garden, directly behind Stacy's truck.

She signaled for Lewis to stay where he was while she and Graydon got out. It seemed odd to her that the mention of his grandfather had made him so sad.

"I'm sorry. I didn't know you and Nate were close. I shouldn't have brought the subject up. Believe me, I wasn't trying to criticize you by comparison," Stacy vowed.

He approached, stood close to her and raked his fingers through his hair. "You didn't do anything wrong. It's me. I had a rough…week." Yeah, he added silently. *All* the weeks and years were rough until I finally found out the truth. Nathan couldn't accept me as his son because he wasn't my actual father! And there was nothing I could do to change that fact.

"There is a lot of stress going around," Stacy agreed with a faint smile.

She started to extend her hand in parting just as Gray reached to clasp her upper arms. The sensation of his gentle grasp was enough to make her sway slightly.

He steadied her and spoke softly, intimately. "I want to thank you again for coming so quickly. I was pretty worried when Mother called to say she'd lost track of Missy."

"I know. It's all right. I'm glad everything turned out so well." She sighed and glanced into the back seat of the car. Lewis had followed her orders to remain still and Missy was draped across his body as if he were a furry beanbag chair.

"It might not have ended so well without you." Gray took a deep, ragged breath. "If anything had happened to Missy, I don't know what I'd have done."

Touched by his obvious fondness for the child, Stacy reached up and patted his cheek to comfort him. "It's all right. She's safe now. That's all that matters."

"You're right. Thanks." He bent to place a chaste goodbye kiss on her forehead.

Stacy nearly swooned. Before she could catch her breath, she heard a loud gasp from the nearby rose garden.

Graydon heard it, too. He held firm to her arms and drew her closer. Leaning down, he whispered, "Mother."

"Oh, no!" She felt like a teenager, caught necking behind the high school science building. Not that she'd ever done anything like that.

Gray was amused. "Oh, yes."

"Then let go of me!" Stacy pushed her palms against his chest but he didn't budge.

"Are you sure that's what you want?"

His voice was so quiet she could barely hear what he said. Wide-eyed, she leaned back to look up into his eyes. They twinkled with mischief.

She managed a weak, "What?"

Gray blessed her with a lopsided smile. "I just thought maybe we should give my mother something more to think about, that's all."

Stacy watched him bending closer, tilting his head. His warm, sweet breath reminded her of chocolate ice cream. She had an almost irresistible urge to stand on her tiptoes and kiss him.

You can't do that, even if you want to! she told herself.

But she needn't have worried about making a decision one way or the other. Gray made it for her. Leaning closer, he gently brushed her lips with his, then pulled her into his embrace, laid her back over his arm with a theatrical flourish and proceeded to kiss her as if they were the most romantic couple in the world.

In the background, Estelle Payne gave a strangled shriek. It was accompanied by a man's coarse guffaw.

Gray straightened, steadied Stacy on her feet and loosened his hold. Looking in the direction of the sound he saw his mother scurrying away carrying a basket of fresh-cut flowers. Euless Feeters was standing among the roses, chortling heartily.

The old man raised his fist in the air, thumb up, and hollered, "Way to go, boy!"

Gray couldn't believe what had just happened. All he'd intended to do was tease his mother. He certainly hadn't meant the kiss to seem so real. So earth-shattering. So wonderful!

He looked down at Stacy, certain she'd be upset, if not downright irate. To his surprise she looked as thunderstruck as he felt. Maybe more.

He cleared his throat, stepped back and stuffed his hands into his pockets. "I—I'm sorry. I didn't mean..."

Dizzy, she drew a shaky breath. Never had anyone else's kiss affected her the way Gray's had. Too bad he'd only kissed her to play a joke on his pretentious mother. Well, if *he* was sorry about their kiss, then she would claim the same negative reaction, providing she could muster enough common sense to convince herself it was true before speaking up. She finally chanced it. "That was totally uncalled for, Mr. Payne."

"I know. That's why I said I was sorry." A wry smile lifted one corner of his mouth. "It did have the desired effect, though."

"Oh? And what might that be?" Stacy couldn't help the resentment that crept into her voice. She'd just received the most extraordinary kiss of her lifetime and he was making jokes about it as if it didn't matter at all.

"My mother, of course. Did you see her flounce off? It was hilarious."

See her? Even now, Stacy could barely concentrate, let alone see straight. Disgusted with herself she covered her weakness with cynicism and cited an analogy that was anything but romantic. "No. You had me hanging upside down over your arm like a dead chicken. How did you expect me to see anything from that position?"

His eyebrows arched but he didn't comment on her choice of example. "Yeah, well..."

Stacy made a show of straightening her clothing even though she wasn't mussed, then turned toward the car. "I really should be going. Do you want to lift Missy off Lewis so he doesn't wake her when I let him get up?"

"Sure." Gray's hand hesitated on the door handle. "Just tell him not to bite me, okay?"

"You're lucky I told him to stay in the car in the first place," she countered, "or you'd probably be nursing a sore ankle and counting his teeth marks right now."

He chuckled. "No doubt. And in this case, I'd deserve every mark."

"I'm glad to hear we agree." Circling the car, Stacy opened the opposite door, leaned in, and laid her hand on Lewis's head to steady him while Gray lifted Missy away. The man's outlandish caution

HOW TO VALIDATE
YOUR
EDITOR'S FREE GIFT!
"THANK YOU"

1. Peel off the FREE GIFTS SEAL from front cover. Place it in the space provided at right. This automatically entitles you to receive two free books and an exciting mystery gift.

2. Send back this card and you'll get 2 Love Inspired® novels. These books have a combined cover price of $9.00 in the U.S. and $10.50 in Canada, but they are yours to keep absolutely FREE!

3. There's no catch. You're under no obligation to buy anything. We charge nothing—ZERO—for your first shipment. And you don't have to make any minimum number of purchases—not even one!

4. We call this line Love Inspired because each month you'll receive novels that are filled with joy, faith and true Christian values. The stories will lift your spirits and gladden your heart! You'll like the convenience of getting them delivered to your home well before they are in stores. And you'll like our discount prices too!

5. We hope that after receiving your free books you'll want to remain a subscriber. But the choice is yours—to continue or cancel, anytime at all! So why not take us up on our invitation, with no risk of any kind. You'll be glad you did!

6. Don't forget to detach your FREE BOOKMARK. And remember... just for validating your Editor's Free Gift Offer, we'll send you 2 novels and a gift, *ABSOLUTELY FREE!*

YOURS FREE!

We'll send you a fabulous mystery gift absolutely FREE, simply for accepting our no-risk offer!

PLACE
FREE GIFTS
SEAL
HERE

YES! I have placed my Editor's "thank you" Free Gifts seal in the space provided above. Please send me the 2 FREE books and gift for which I qualify. I understand that I am under no obligation to purchase anything further, as explained on the opposite page.

303 IDL CQEM

103 IDL CQEN
(LI-EC-01/00)

NAME (PLEASE PRINT CLEARLY)

ADDRESS

APT.#   CITY

STATE/PROV.   ZIP/POSTAL CODE

Thank You!

If offer card is missing, write to: Steeple Hill Reader Service, 3010 Walden Ave., P.O. Box 1867, Buffalo, NY 14240-1867

BUSINESS REPLY MAIL
FIRST-CLASS MAIL   PERMIT NO. 717   BUFFALO, NY

POSTAGE WILL BE PAID BY ADDRESSEE

STEEPLE HILL READER SERVICE
3010 WALDEN AVE
PO BOX 1867
BUFFALO NY 14240-9952

NO POSTAGE
NECESSARY
IF MAILED
IN THE
UNITED STATES

with regard to the usually mild-tempered dog was amusing.

Gray shot her a contrite glance, then spoke quietly to keep from waking the child. "In the future, I'll be much more careful, I promise."

"Let's hope so." The words didn't fit Stacy's innermost feelings but she refused to give him the satisfaction of knowing how deeply she'd been affected by his casual kiss.

Missy stirred. Gray laid a finger on his lips. "Shush. I didn't mean to make you mad. I just thought—"

"What? That it would be fun to shock your mother by kissing someone from the wrong side of the tracks? Well, it worked. And now that you've had your fun, I'll be going. Come, Lewis."

She turned away quickly to hide her vulnerable nature and reddening cheeks, and led the dog to her truck. If Gray suspected how much his so-called joke had embarrassed her, not to mention how she was still trembling from his touch, he'd have even more to chuckle about. She wasn't about to provide cheap amusement for the Payne family. Let them look down their highbrow noses. She didn't care. Her peers had been belittling her since her teens because she didn't have at least one parent like the rest of them. She was used to that kind of treatment.

Thoughtful, she slid behind the wheel. She'd never forget the times her foster parents had sent her to school in worn-out hand-me-down clothes and she'd been the brunt of cruel remarks over which she'd had no control.

But she'd survived. And eventually flourished. If she was guilty of reverse discrimination, as Graydon claimed, she'd work on overcoming that character fault. But she wasn't going to subject herself to any more humiliation at the hands of the Paynes.

Enough was enough.

Gray called ahead to tell his brother he was bringing Missy home. All the way there he thought about Stacy. About the first time he'd met her.

She'd been barely eighteen when Mark had arranged for her to meet his family. It was clear from the moment she'd set foot in the grand house that she was way out of her element. Her beautiful eyes had grown wide. Her lips had parted slightly in amazement. To her credit, she'd stood tall and faced the elder Paynes with as much grace as any untutored girl could be expected to display.

Every minute of that evening was imprinted in Gray's memory. Stacy had smiled too wide, laughed too loudly, cared too much. She was enchanting, yet naive. Eager to please, yet totally clueless. By the end of the long, tedious dinner they'd all shared, Gray had made up his mind she'd never survive the rigors of trying to belong to his family. If the effort didn't crush her spirit, it would change her into the kind of person she wouldn't purposely choose to be.

He'd tried to make Mark see the problems inherent in marrying Stacy. His younger brother had merely laughed off his concern, recognizing no contrast between Stacy and any other girl he'd ever dated.

To Gray, there was all the difference in the world. This girl was more than just pretty. She was sensitive, innocent, inexperienced. And she had a heart that spoke to his; that cried out for love and acceptance. He didn't have any tangible reasons for what he did next. He just knew he couldn't stand by and let her marry Mark.

And she hadn't.

Mark was pacing in front of the house when Gray pulled into the drive. He leaned out the car window. "Where's Candace?"

"Still out shopping. She should be home in a couple of hours." Mark leaned down to peer into the back seat of the BMW. "What's going on? Why are you bringing the kid back so early? I had to leave a pile of work on my desk and cancel two meetings after you called."

"Didn't Mother tell you?"

"Tell me what?" Mark shrugged. "The last I heard, Melissa was at the folks' place."

"She was." Reaching into the back seat, Gray undid the groggy little girl's seat belt and lifted her gently out of the car. One of her thin arms wrapped around his neck.

Mark led the way toward the house. "Well, I

guess you'd better bring her in. I don't know what I'm going to do with her till Candace gets back. This adoption business was her idea. I don't know a thing about kids.''

''They're just like real people,'' Gray said cynically. ''You know, with feelings and needs. The usual.''

''Very funny.'' Mark cast a disgusted glance over his shoulder. ''You still haven't told me why you're here.''

Gray's hold on the child tightened protectively. ''Remember the hidden closet under the stairs where you and I used to hide from our math tutor?''

''Vaguely. Why?''

''Because that's where Missy went. Only the door stuck shut and she couldn't get back out. If it hadn't been for Stacy and her dog—''

Mark interrupted. ''Wait just a second. Are you saying that *Mother* called Stacy?''

''Not a chance. I did. And she came right away, even though she'd been up all night and was dead tired.''

Following his brother through the house to a back bedroom, Gray laid Missy on her bed without waking her. As soon as he straightened he gestured toward the door. ''Come on. You and I need to have a talk.''

He knew his brother wouldn't argue. They'd established their pecking order early in life and only their sister, Rosalie, had ever challenged Gray's authority. Now that she was living half a world away, there was no chance she'd intercede the way she used to. That gave Gray a distinct advantage; one he intended to press.

Leading Mark into the den Gray seated himself casually on the Moroccan leather sofa, his legs outstretched in a pose of utter confidence. He pointed to a nearby chair. "Sit."

The younger man gave a nervous laugh. "You've been spending too much time hanging around Stacy. You're starting to sound like a dog trainer."

"I wish it were that easy to get through to you," Gray said. "Are you going to sit down or do you intend to stand there all day?"

"I'll sit. Mind if I smoke?"

"It's bad for Missy."

Mark laid the pack aside. "Okay. You've made your point." His sigh was audible. "I never dreamed there'd be so many changes when we started a family."

"I suppose it is harder when the child's half-grown. But that doesn't alter the fact that you have a personal responsibility for your daughter. You can't leave it all to your wife. When the adoption goes through, you'll be as much Missy's father as if you'd sired her yourself."

Mark was shaking his head. "Not according to Dad, I won't. He's already making noises about wanting a *real* grandson to carry on the Payne name. You're lucky you're not married or he'd be after you, too."

"I doubt it." Gritting his teeth, Gray dealt with his negative reaction. Some things never changed, did they? Neither did some people. It was a shame Nathan had never been able to view him as his real son. He'd turned his problems with his father over to the Lord long ago, when he'd first become a Christian, but that didn't mean that the old man's unfair opinions had stopped hurting.

"Have you and Candace decided to give up trying to have a baby?" Gray asked.

"No. She's still going to doctors to see if they can fix whatever's wrong. I guess she just got tired of waiting and worrying. I went along with the adoption because she wanted it so badly." He shrugged. "It'll all work out. As long as my wife is happy, I'm happy."

"What about Missy?"

"What about her? She's got a nice home, plenty of toys, food on the table and anything else she needs. I don't understand why she keeps causing so much trouble. Doesn't she know we're trying to help her?"

"According to Stacy, probably not," Gray said. "Which reminds me, why didn't you tell me Stacy was orphaned when she was just a kid?"

"And have you blab it to our parents? No way. I was having enough trouble getting along with them back then. I didn't intend to give them any more reasons to tell me I was a fool." Leaning forward, he rested his elbows on his knees and spread his hands. "Anyway, it all worked out. Stacy saw the futility of our relationship and broke it off. Saved me from doing it."

"You never knew why, did you?" Gray shook his head slowly, sadly, remembering all too well. "I suppose it's time I told you. I had a little brotherly talk with your girlfriend and explained how she would never fit into our family." He steeled himself, waiting for Mark's temper to flare. It didn't take long.

The younger man jumped to his feet, his face florid with rage. "You what!"

"I scared her off. It's a simple as that."

Mark's hands were balled into tight fists. "How *dare* you interfere in my life like that? What made you think you had the right?"

Frowning, Gray faced him. "I didn't do it for *you.* I did it for Stacy. She was young and way too kindhearted. She didn't know what she was getting into. But *I* knew. I'd been there. If she'd stayed, Dad would have chewed her up and spit out the pieces. And if that hadn't been enough to break her spirit, our mother would have managed to make her feel like something that had crawled out from under a rock."

"So you sent her packing? Just like that? I ought to break you in half!"

"You'd probably be justified in trying," Gray said. "If it's any consolation, I've regretted what I did ever since."

"How comforting. And that's supposed to make it all right?"

"No. But it's the best I can do. There was no way I could stand by and let a sweet girl like Stacy be hurt."

"So, you played God with my life, is that it?"

Gray reached out to his brother, disheartened when Mark backed away. "If you'll calm down and think about it, you'll realize I did both you and Stacy a favor."

"Oh, sure. And now, you've decided to romance her yourself, right? How convenient."

Gray was taken aback. "Everything I said about our family goes for me, too, Mark. Especially now that I've gotten to know Stacy better. I'd never subject her to the ordeal of becoming a Payne."

"But you have thought about it, haven't you?"

Gray refused to consider what his honest answer should be. "I told you years ago, I'm not the marrying kind. Never have been. Never will be. I leave the romance up to you."

"And all the grandsons to carry on the family name?" Mark's eyebrows raised to punctuate the question.

"*Especially* them."

"Mother won't like hearing you say that."

A twinge of regret touched Gray's heart. He quickly dismissed it. "It was her decision to marry a Payne. She should have to live with the consequences. I do."

Frowning, Mark studied his older brother. "Stop

talking nonsense. I know you and the old man had a fight when you turned down the job he offered you, but that doesn't mean he's given up on you.''

Gray refused to be baited. In time, perhaps he'd tell Mark what had transpired when Nathan and he had argued so vehemently. And perhaps not. Baring his soul wouldn't change a thing. Neither would walking away from his family for good and hurting his mother. In spite of everything that had happened, he did love her.

''Enough about me,'' Gray said flatly. ''What are you going to do about that unhappy little girl?''

''Still meddling in my life, dear brother? I thought you'd learned your lesson.''

''Cut the sarcasm and answer my question.'' Muscles clenching, he stood firm and stared Mark down, relieved when the childhood tactic still worked.

''What *can* I do?'' Mark grumbled.

''Well, you could start by spending more time with Missy. Get to know her. Talk to her.''

''Oh, sure. I don't know what to say to kids.''

''Then try just listening. The kid needs to feel like you care, like she can actually belong here. And while you're at it, don't dump her at Dad's again for a while.''

''Why not? I thought Mother wanted me to.''

''She wants whatever Dad tells her she wants. You know that. That's how it's always been with them.''

''Now you're starting to sound like Rosalie.''

"Heaven forbid. Our sister is not exactly the most open-minded person I've ever met."

"No, but she did have it out with the old man before she married Stan and ran off to Paris."

"She did?" Gray scowled. "What happened?"

"I don't know. I assume Stan was the problem. Rosie was crying so hard I couldn't make out most of what she said. She and Dad argued and the next morning, she was gone. Just like that. Mother was devastated."

"I wonder why she never told me all that?"

"Probably because you and Dad were already on the outs and she didn't want to make things worse. Mom has always played the peacemaker. She may have her faults but she knows when to keep her mouth shut." Mark glared at him. "Unlike someone else I could mention."

"I only try to do what's right."

Nodding, his brother said, "Yeah. I know. Do me a favor, will you? Don't try to tell me how to live my life. My nerves can't take much more of your so-called help."

Chapter Nine

During the days that followed, Stacy managed to put the Payne family out of her mind—for the most part. As long as she kept busy, she seldom relived her visit to the estate or let herself dwell on the effects of Graydon's kiss.

Nights, however, were a different story. In the quiet of the evening, when all her chores were done, the whippoorwill was calling and lightning bugs rose out of the long grass to blink fluorescent green in their search for a mate, Stacy always grew pensive.

This night was no different. She couldn't prevent her thoughts from returning to the last time she'd been with the enigmatic man who had changed the course of her life.

What might she have been like if she'd married Mark, as she'd once imagined? Stacy knew she wouldn't be the same person she now was. Instead of leaning on someone else she'd built a successful career all by herself. She smiled. Well, not quite by herself. The good Lord had directed her, sent encouragement when she needed it and led her to the best dogs for the job so she could offer the kind of assistance for which she'd become well-known.

Which just went to prove that God could use *anybody*. Even her. Even a man like Graydon Payne. The comparison made her edgy. He'd certainly made a jumble of her feelings when he'd kissed her. Every time she smelled a rose she flashed back to their encounter in Estelle's garden. For a joke, the kiss had certainly seemed genuine enough. At least it had to her.

Which was why Stacy was so mad at herself. It was disgusting to realize she didn't have enough sense to separate fantasy from reality. Maybe that was because she'd been forced to grow up so quickly after the accident. Or maybe it was because she'd never had one of those private, mother-daughter talks the other girls had giggled about when she was in school.

Caught up in the sudden urge to unburden herself, she reached for the phone and dialed the Spring River Campground. When Judy answered, Stacy said, "Hi. It's me. I'm looking for a little motherly advice. Are you up for that?"

Judy chuckled. "Sure. I'll be your mama. As long as I don't have to baby you. How are you, anyway? We haven't heard a peep from you since you were here."

"I'm fine. Sort of." Stacy grimaced in disgust. "I know I've neglected you and Angie. I mean well. I make myself all kinds of promises, then as soon as I get back to work, I push so hard I forget all about my friends. I'm really sorry."

"Apology accepted. When are you coming to see us?"

"I can't do it this week. I have a speech to give in Little Rock on Saturday, which I haven't written yet. Then there's church on Sunday. By Monday I have to get ready to teach a class of new volunteers."

"When does the class start?" Judy asked wisely.

"On the thirteenth. Why?"

"Because that's nearly two weeks away. You have lots of time to come see us again, if you really want to. Then you and I can talk face-to-face. We mamas like to be able to look our daughters in the eye and make sure they're telling us the whole truth. At least that's how my mom was. She could tell in a heartbeat whether or not I was being honest."

Stacy sighed. "I wish I could remember more about my mother. Sometimes, I'll recall a whole event from when we were together. Other times, the best I can do is look at her picture and imagine what she must have been like."

"I know what you mean," Judy said soberly. "I feel that way about my grandmother. She died when I was seven. When I try to remember her just as she was, the details are all fuzzy.'' She paused, then added, ''When can we expect you?''

''I don't know if I can break away.''

''Phooey. Just do it.''

''But my dogs need care and training and—''

Judy interrupted. ''Get somebody to come in and feed for you. The poor dogs probably need a vacation from you as much as you need one from them. Give everybody a break. Cut loose. Run away to the mountains and relax.''

''Run away?'' Stacy accented her words with a humph of disgust. ''I've done that. Don't you remember what happened when we were in high school? I took off and was gone for days before they found me and brought me back. I almost got sent back to jail.''

''Jail?'' Judy's voice was squeaky. ''I didn't know you were ever in jail. What did you do?''

''Absolutely nothing criminal,'' Stacy assured her. ''I was just a very unhappy teenager because I had no real family to support me.''

''I had a great family and I was still miserable,'' Judy confessed. ''I think that's part of growing up. We all go through it. At least you turned out all right.''

Did I? Stacy wondered to herself. ''I don't know. Sometimes, it seems like there must be more—like there's something important missing from my life. Know what I mean?''

''Important, as in a *man?*''

Stacy was quick to deny it. "No! Of course not. I don't even have time for the friends I've already got. There's no room in my life for romance. You know that."

"Okay. So, when shall we expect you?"

"You're not going to take no for an answer, are you?"

"Nope. You obviously need a break. Take one before you fall apart. Mother's orders."

"Yes, Mother. Bake me a nice apple pie, will you? I promise I'll be there as soon as I can get my chores farmed out to the neighbor boy who usually helps me. The speech is day after tomorrow. I'll pack before I go to Little Rock and drive to your place directly from there."

"Sounds good to me. How about bringing some ice cream for the top of the pie?"

"It's a deal. Anything else you need?"

"My old friend," Judy said sincerely.

"Hey. Watch it with the *old* part, will you? I'm only twenty-nine." Hesitating, she added, "Going on sixteen, if my latest adventure is any indication."

"Oooh, sounds interesting. Hurry and get here so we can hear all about it."

"Right." Bidding her goodbye, Stacy wondered if she was making a mistake by even thinking of airing her confusing feelings in regard to Graydon Payne. As girls, she, Angela and Judy had discussed many private problems without serious repercussions, but that didn't mean they'd be able to

understand her now. None of them were kids anymore. And potential relationships were no longer
something to giggle about after class behind the
gym.

Stacy huffed in disdain. There was no way that
Graydon Payne had meant to be romantic when he
kissed her, any more than she intended to be gul-
lible enough to take him seriously. Surely, the Lord
wouldn't expect her to forgive him for everything
he'd done in the past simply because she happened
to find him mildly attractive now?

She knew she should turn to God in fervent
prayer; ask Him what to do, what to think, how to
behave in the present dilemma. But she decided
not to. She didn't want to take the chance that her
Heavenly Father might actually want to influence
her in Graydon's favor.

It was bad enough going against what her innermost heart kept insisting it wanted. She wasn't
going to acknowledge that God might be on Graydon's side in the matter, too.

The hotel banquet room in Little Rock was only
half full when Stacy smoothed her pale-blue silk
dress and stood up to begin her lecture on the
tracking dog program. Rather than let the disap-
pointing turnout influence her attitude, she reminded herself that her wealthy, venerable host
knew precisely which philanthropists to invite to
gain the most financial support for her program.
Having the *right* people there was far more im-

portant than having the room full of disinterested folks who'd just come for a free lunch.

She smiled and introduced herself, then began citing some of the specific successes with which she'd been directly involved, either as an instructor or as a member of a search party. Usually, she enjoyed describing the training program and its benefits. This time her mind kept drifting to her upcoming getaway and the freedom from daily responsibility. She hadn't realized how stressed she was until she'd made the arrangements to take some time off.

Anxious to be on her way, Stacy concluded her speech and prepared to leave the podium while her host waited for the applause to die down so he could take over the plea for funds. A deep, male voice coming from the very back of the room stopped her in midmotion.

"You forgot to mention one of your most recent cases," he called.

The assembled guests pivoted to see who was speaking. Stacy didn't have to look. She knew it was Graydon Payne. The fine hairs on the back of her neck were prickling and her lovely luncheon salad lay bunched in her stomach like coarse, dry straw stuffed into the torso of a scarecrow.

"I couldn't possibly list everything." Hoping she sounded more calm than she felt, she addressed the whole group. "The tracking dog program was begun many years ago, long before I became involved. Its continued success, however, depends on the support of benefactors such as yourselves. Now, if you'll excuse me..."

Before she could gather her papers and slide them back into her briefcase, Gray had made his way to the head table and joined her.

He picked up the microphone and began to explain why he'd come. "Ms. Lucas and her dogs saved a close member of my family not once, but twice. When I phoned her to express my gratitude and was told she would be speaking here today, I crashed the party in order to add my support to that of the rest of you."

Gray reached into the breast pocket of his navy-blue suit coat and withdrew an envelope. Instead of handing it to Stacy, however, he passed it to the gentleman who had sponsored her presentation. "I'm sure everyone here will want to contribute, also. Believe me, I've seen these rescue dogs in action and the job they do is amazing."

The man opened the envelope. When he saw the check his gray eyebrows arched in evident surprise. "Thank you, Mr. Payne. This is very generous. I'm sure this will inspire others to give liberally, as well." He extended his hand.

Graydon nodded politely and shook the man's hand. He'd accomplished his purpose. He should be satisfied. Only for some reason, he wasn't. Seeing Stacy again had left him feeling strangely bereft, as if there were some intangible element missing from his life. It was not a frame of mind he enjoyed. On the contrary, the unsettling mood was one he intended to banish as soon as possible.

Which meant he'd simply make a personal apology to Stacy for overstepping the bounds of common courtesy and kissing her, then be on his way. That should be enough to salve his conscience and give him back his peace of mind, since his donation to her training program hadn't done the trick.

Gray turned to speak to her, to invite her to join him for coffee so they could talk privately. To his surprise and chagrin, she'd left the room.

Stacy hurried to the elevator. Glancing over her shoulder she was relieved to see that no one had followed her when she'd slipped out of the banquet hall. Good. Now, all she had to do was ride the elevator to the hotel parking garage, get her truck and she'd be on her way in spite of Graydon's pretentious interruption of her lecture.

The doors slid open. Stacy stepped into the elevator and punched the button for the basement garage. Just as the doors were closing she saw Graydon burst out into the lobby and hurriedly scan the crowd. For an instant, she thought he hadn't seen her. The last glimpse of his penetrating gaze before the doors slammed shut told her she was wrong.

It was the color of her dress that caught his eye. It matched the striking blue of her eyes and set them off as if both had been painted when God had dipped his brush into the summer sky.

Until now, Gray had never seen Stacy in anything but her work clothes. It shouldn't have been a surprise to him that she was so lovely, since that was the overall impression he'd always gotten, yet everything about her had dazzled him when he'd walked into that banquet room and caught sight of her.

Noting that she'd boarded a descending elevator he guessed she was headed for the garage. By taking the stairs two at a time he reached it a few seconds before she did.

He skidded to a stop in front of the elevator as the doors slid open with a whoosh.

Stacy stood very still and stared at him, then found her voice. "How did you do that?"

"Do…what…?" He was struggling to catch his breath.

"Never mind. I know. I just didn't think anybody could run that fast."

Gray managed a lopsided smile. "I imagine it's easier going down than it is going up."

"Undoubtedly." Acting on impulse, she reached for the buttons and punched the closest one.

Before the doors could close again, he jumped aboard. Stacy was too surprised to react in time to get off.

Leaning against the side nearest the controls, he looked terribly proud of himself for having bested her.

Provoked, she said, "I don't suppose you'd be willing to stop this thing and let me off, would you?"

"Sure. As soon as you promise you'll have coffee with me so we can talk."

"We have nothing to talk about. I don't care how much money you gave the rescue tracking program, you can't buy my time. I have too little of it to spare as it is."

"Boy, I know the feeling." He folded his arms across his chest, checked his watch and tried to look nonchalant. "I'm supposed to be in Conway in an hour. I'd hate to miss an important appointment."

"Then you obviously don't have time for coffee, either."

"You're right. How about dinner some time this week? I'm free most nights."

"Well, I'm not," she stated. "As a matter of fact, I'm going to be out of town. I'm leaving immediately." She didn't like the self-satisfied look that appeared on his face, or the knowing glint in his eyes.

"Ah, that explains it."

"Explains what?" Stacy was getting more and more frustrated at not knowing why he was acting so smug.

"The camping gear I saw in your truck when I was first looking for you. I wondered what you were up to."

"What I do and where I go is none of your business."

"Unless I happen to need your services again," Gray countered. "Suppose Missy runs away while you're gone?"

"Then you'll have to call someone else. The boy who's watching my place for me has the phone numbers of other members of the search team. He'll be glad to refer you."

"I don't want somebody else. Missy trusts you and Lewis. If we have more problems with her, you're the one who should go after her. Otherwise she might hide and never be found." His smile spread. "Besides, I want to get my money's worth and you're the best."

That did it. Stacy was at the end of her patience. She lunged for the elevator controls. He blocked her effort with his body and she accidentally hit the red, emergency stop button instead of a closer floor, as she'd intended.

Bells went off. The elevator came to an abrupt halt. Stacy was already off balance. Her high-heel shoes made her stagger and she blundered into Gray before she could regain her footing.

He caught her easily. "What did you do that for?"

"Let me go."

"Okay. Whatever you say." He opened his arms with a broad flourish. "What do you propose we do, now?"

"Why ask me?" The bells were still sounding,

increasing Stacy's already considerable distress. She clapped her hands over her ears.

"Because you're the one who got us stranded," Gray shouted over the din. He was grinning broadly.

"It's not funny."

"I think it is."

She pulled a face. "You would."

"Don't worry. I'm sure somebody will hear the alarm and come to our rescue," he said calmly. "In the meantime, we can have our little chat."

The noise stopped abruptly. Stacy slowly uncovered her ears. "I don't want to chat. I don't want to be stuck in here with you. And I don't want to have anything more to do with you once we get out of this mess. Is that clear?"

"Very." He couldn't get over how cute she looked, standing there with her fists on her hips, insisting on having her own way. "I don't suppose you'd like to hear my apology again, would you? I've rehearsed it a lot and it's much more convincing than it was when we were out by my mother's rose garden."

Stacy rolled her eyes. "Please. Don't remind me. I've never been so embarrassed in my life."

"I have. But I probably get around more than you do. For instance, there was the time I'd arranged for an extravagant steak dinner to impress an influential client. I didn't find out he was a strict vegetarian until after it was all over."

"He didn't say anything at the time?"

"Not much. I think he was too busy feeling sorry for his dinner. On a personal level."

"That's terrible." She couldn't help the slight smile that lifted the corners of her mouth. "Poor man. I take it you didn't impress him the way you'd hoped?"

"Well, he didn't hire me as his consultant, if that's what you mean. I doubt he'll ever forget me, though."

"No kidding." Neither would she, Stacy admitted. Her first dose of the Paynes, with Mark, hadn't left her nearly as affected as getting to know Graydon had.

The elevator came to life and started to ascend. Gray realized time was running out. He chose to use their last few moments of forced togetherness to reiterate his regret for having caused her embarrassment. "Okay. If you won't have dinner with me, I guess I have no choice. I'll try to make this quick. I really am sorry, Stacy. I didn't mean to give the impression I was only kissing you because I knew it would aggravate my mother."

"You weren't?" Her eyes widened.

"Well, yes, I was. But I didn't intend to humiliate you. I thought you'd enjoy driving Mother crazy as much as I would. I never dreamed you'd think I was just using you."

"That's exactly what you were doing."

"No, it isn't. I thought we were having fun. You know. Kidding around. Letting off a little steam after the harrowing afternoon we'd all had."

Stacy shook her head sadly. "You still don't see the truth, do you?"

"Maybe it isn't me who can't accept candor and honesty."

Upward movement stopped. The door slid open to reveal a middle-aged, balding technician in a grey-striped jumpsuit that was too tight around his waist.

He eyed the two people in the elevator car with suspicion. "Everything all right in there, folks?"

"Fine," Gray said. "We hit the red button by mistake."

The man chuckled. "Sure, sure. I know how it is. I was young once, too. Next time y'all want some privacy, though, do me a favor and go park somewhere instead of messing with my elevators. It throws the whole schedule off when I have a car go down like this."

"It was an accident," Stacy insisted.

"Is that a fact?" The technician boarded the elevator as they got off and held the safety switch so the door would stay open. "Well, maybe so. This is the first time I've had it happen where the lovers spent all their time talkin' about kissin' instead of fixin' to do it."

Stacy felt hot color rise in her cheeks. "What?"

The man chuckled as he pointed to the roof of the car. "We've got a camera and a mike mounted up there for security reasons. You two sure fight a lot. Maybe you ain't right for each other."

Gray began to roar with laughter the same way

he had when he'd promised his mother he'd keep Stacy from stealing the family silver.

To her credit, Stacy joined in. She was still chuckling to herself when she walked down the stairs from the lobby to the parking garage. Thanks to Graydon Payne, it was going to be a long time before she was prepared to board another elevator.

Or smell another rose.

Chapter Ten

The drive from Little Rock to Judy and Angela's Spring River camp took Stacy three long hours. By the time she arrived she'd visualized her most recent encounter with Gray a hundred times. Each time she replayed the incident she remembered different elements.

What she yearned to do was focus only on the negative. Unfortunately, that was proving impossible. She kept seeing his smile and the whimsical twinkle in his eyes, kept hearing his engrossing laugh.

Finally, she gave in and sought divine help. "Father? I've got a problem," she said softly as she wheeled into the drive that led to the main camp. "I don't want to be interested in Gray but I can't help myself. I actually like him. He's good-looking, funny and pretty understanding, considering.'' Instantly, his opinion about her uncon-scious discrimination against the wealthy came to mind.

"Maybe *too* understanding," she added. "And it's so sweet how he loves that poor, lonely little girl."

Was that why she felt so drawn to the man? she wondered. Was it because he reminded her of how lost and alone she'd felt when she was in a situa-tion similar to Missy's? Perhaps. If only God would explain it all.

"Please, Father," Stacy pled. "I'm so confused about everything. Help me? Please?"

Falling silent, she completed her prayer the way she'd been taught, then waited for an answer. No bolt of divine lightning struck to illuminate her hazy thoughts. No sense of peace descended the way she'd hoped it would. Truth to tell, she felt more out of sorts than she had before she'd re-sorted to calling on the Lord.

Stacy chewed on her lower lip. She'd experi-enced that uncomfortable state more than once since becoming a Christian. In the past, those feel-ings had meant she was out of fellowship with God. If that were the case this time, chances were the hindrance was due to Graydon Payne and his pompous family.

"But what am I supposed to *do* about it?" Stacy grumbled as she parked her truck and climbed out.

Judy ran to greet her with a welcoming hug. "Hi! How did things go in Little Rock?"

"Oh, fine."

"You don't seem convinced." She let go and stepped back. "Wanna tell Mama all about it?"

Stacy's guilty conscience reared its head. She grimaced. "I'm not real sure that's a good idea."

"Uh-oh. I sense an all-nighter coming." Judy reached into the truck to help her carry her things up to the cabin. "Good thing I talked Angie into baking two pies. We'll need our nourishment if we're going to stay awake."

"Oh, no!" Stacy stopped. "I forgot to bring the ice cream."

"That's okay. You probably had other things on your mind." Judy was watching her closely. "Am I right?"

Stacy made a silly, self-deprecating face. "Mama," she gibed, "you know me far too well."

Graydon had worked out with weights and even jogged an extra mile after dinner to tire himself out, but he still couldn't sleep. It was ridiculous to be so determined to make Stacy Lucas accept him, yet that was the notion that refused to leave his mind, refused to let him relax enough to doze off.

He could understand why she was put off by his family, his father in particular. She didn't owe Nathan any loyalty the way he did. Or the way his mother did.

For his entire childhood Gray had wondered what it was that made him feel like an outsider within his own family. He'd done his best to make his parents proud; gotten good grades in school, stayed out of trouble, played the sports his father appreciated, even considered following Nathan into the family business.

In a way, he was glad he'd had the courage to step out on his own and fend for himself. If he hadn't, he might never have found out what had happened to create the dysfunctional family relationships he'd had to deal with all his life.

The memory was still as clear as if the confrontation had taken place mere days ago instead of years. It rose unbidden to fill his mind once again.

That day, Nathan had been practicing his golf putting in the den. Gray had chosen to use that occasion to approach his father about his plans for the future, now that he'd finished college.

He'd knocked at the open door to get the older man's attention. "Hi, Dad. You busy?"

"Busy enough." Nathan had kept his concentration focused on the golf ball. "Your mother tells me you're graduating with honors."

"Yes, sir." Not a word was said about paternal pride in his accomplishments but Gray was so used to that kind of reaction he easily let it pass.

"Good. Looks like I'll have to be getting your name painted on a door at the office pretty soon." Still, Nathan didn't face him.

"Well, sir, that's what I wanted to talk to you about," Gray said boldly. "You know how much I appreciate the opportunity but—"

"Spit it out, boy."

"Okay. I've done so well in architecture and city planning, I've decided to start my own consulting firm. I know it's a gamble but a couple of friends and I have worked out the details and we have the necessary skills. It's what we want to do."

When Nathan finally straightened and looked at him, Gray was astounded by his cold expression. He'd suspected his father would be disappointed in his choice of career but he hadn't expected the clear contempt mirrored in the older man's eyes.

"I knew all along it wouldn't work," Nathan said.

"I beg your pardon?" Gray was confused and more than a little uncomfortable. His father had always been distant. Open animosity, however, was a new phenomenon.

"It's because of that religious nut you had for a roommate in college, isn't it? He's convinced you that you don't owe me a thing. Right?"

"James had nothing to do with it," Gray countered. "This was my decision."

With a shrug, Nathan had turned away and gone back to his putting. "Fine. It suits me. I wouldn't have even offered you a job in the first place if your mother hadn't insisted. I knew from the first day I saw you that you'd never deserve to become a Payne."

"What?"

"You heard me," he'd said flatly. "You're not my son. You never were."

Even now, Gray could remember every word, every inflection of his father's painful disclosure. He'd run from the room and out into the gardens, so upset he could hardly breathe. That was where his mother had found him and tearfully explained the rest.

"I was young," she'd said. "And in trouble. Your father...I mean, Nathan...said he loved me anyway and didn't care that I was carrying another man's child. If I'd had any idea he'd have so much trouble accepting you once you were born, I'd never have married him."

After that day, it was only because of his mother's pleas for family harmony that Gray had remained on pseudoamiable terms with his father. Lately, he was beginning to suspect that she wished she hadn't begged him to buy the house at nearby Norfork Lake, in addition to his condo. She and Nathan had Rosalie to give them grandchildren, and Mark to carry on the family name. He, on the other hand, was merely an unwanted, constant reminder of the awful mistake his mother had made.

Gray sighed deeply. Funny how things worked out. The estrangement within his family wasn't because of anything he'd done, or not done. Yet his father's critical attitude had almost destroyed him, made him believe the whole world was against him. If it hadn't been for his old friend James, who'd led him to the Lord and shown him the unconditional love of his Heavenly Father, Gray didn't know what kind of person he would have eventually become.

That sobering thought reminded him of Missy. His heart was breaking for her. As her uncle he'd made up his mind to do what he could, but he knew he couldn't take the place of her real father. Nor could Mark. No one could. Not in the way she needed right now.

He could, however, offer her a respite from Candace's unreasonable rules of proper conduct. His sister-in-law meant well. She just didn't have the foggiest idea what Missy was going through or how hard it was for the child to make the adjustment of coming to live with new parents so soon after the loss of her natural father.

All he had to do was convince Mark and Candace that it was for the best that Missy attend an upcoming church camp. He'd already promised to help chaperon, thanks to his old friend James's constant urging, so the situation was tailor-made. Missy could get away from daily stress and he'd be nearby if she got scared and needed him.

It was a perfect plan. Gray just hoped the Lord agreed.

"I don't believe it! You were actually stuck in an elevator with him?" Angie giggled at Stacy, her dark curls jiggling. "Oh, my. What a picture."

Judy agreed. "No kidding. So, what happened next? Did he kiss you, again?"

"Of course not," Stacy said dryly.

"Well, why not? The whole thing sounds like it had to be providential. I've always thought God had a great sense of humor. This just proves it."

Stacy shook her head. "It does not. All it proves is that Graydon Payne is a stubborn, impossible man with an inflated opinion of himself. He actually thought I'd agree to go out to dinner with him. Can you believe it?"

"Well, I never!" Judy huffed dramatically. "Imagine the nerve of the guy. Driving all the way to Little Rock to apologize and support your pet project with an enormous check, and then being so uncouth that he formally asks you to dine with him some evening. Such insolence. Such poor manners."

Dumbfounded, Stacy stared at her friends. "You're saying I was wrong?"

"Not me." Angie immediately jumped to her feet and headed for the kitchen. "I didn't say a thing. You two go ahead and talk. I'll go cut us each a big piece of pie."

"Without ice cream," Judy called after her. "Stacy was so bumfuzzled by her elevator adventure with the incorrigible Mr. Payne she forgot to buy any."

"I was not. I just—"

"Oh, can it. You and I both know you're kidding yourself. You care about the man and you know it. Or you would know it if you'd stop denying your feelings. It's okay to fall in love. Almost everybody does it sometime."

Stacy's mouth gaped. She snapped it shut. "I am *not* in love."

"Okay. Have it your way."

"If I could have things my way, I'd never have met any of the Paynes."

"But you did meet them. Therefore, we have to assume the Lord has a good reason for your continued association with them."

"I do agree with that," Stacy said. "I think He wants me to be in a position to help Missy."

"Fine. Help her. Nothing says you can't help yourself at the same time."

"I don't need any help. Especially not in the romance department. I'm content just as I am. I have my work, my dogs, my friends." She made a face. "Even the ones who disagree with me are a blessing most of the time."

"Good. Glad to hear it," Judy said with a smile. "Then you won't mind my saying I think you're making a big mistake by pushing this guy away."

"I'm not pushing Gray away," Stacy countered. "I'm turning around and running for my life. Believe me, he's the last man I'd ever want to get serious about." To her chagrin, her friend began to chuckle. "What's so funny?"

"You are. You reminded me of that joke about lost keys being found in the last place you look. Of course they are, because once you find them, you stop looking."

"And I said Gray was the last man I'd want to

get serious about." Stacy hoped she hadn't inadvertently spoken a hidden truth. "Wonderful."

"I think he is," Judy said. "If you ever decide to give him away, I'm available."

A frisson of jealousy caught Stacy by surprise. She ignored it. "He's not mine to give. But if he was, you'd be welcome to him."

"Good," Judy teased, "then the next time I see him, I'll tell him you said so."

Stacy snapped her jaw closed again before she could blurt out something else she'd regret. She'd asked for divine guidance and apparently received it. She just didn't happen to like what she'd learned about herself.

It was late when Stacy's conscience finally made up her mind for her. Judy and Angie had both gone to bed, providing the privacy she needed for what she was about to do. She got out Gray's business card, punched in the numbers for his home phone, then listened to the drone of an answering machine on the other end of the line.

When it finished its speech and beeped, she said, "I can't talk to this thing, Gray. I'm up at the camp where Missy got lost the first time." She recited the telephone number. "I'll be here till Friday. I'd appreciate it if you'd call me when you get a chance. I have something important I need to say to you."

She was about to hang up when a sleepy-sounding male voice asked, "How about saying it, now?"

"You're there!"

"No," he bantered, "this is still a machine. I'm an interactive computer."

"In that case," she said sweetly, "I can speak bluntly and no one's feelings will be hurt."

"I don't know. I have some pretty sensitive microchips."

"I'll bet you do." She cleared her throat. The lump of conscience remained. There was nothing to do but begin. "Um...I thought I should call to apologize for my conduct in the elevator, today."

"Yesterday," he corrected. "It's after midnight."

Oh, dear. This whole approach was not going as smoothly as she'd hoped. "I'm sorry. Maybe you'd rather I called back later."

"Not at all. I was up."

That news relieved some of Stacy's guilt for disturbing him until he added, "I had to get up. My phone was ringing."

"Stop that. I'm trying to be serious."

"Sorry. Go ahead. What was it you wanted to say?"

"That I was out of line earlier. I do appreciate your driving all the way into town to support search and rescue the way you did. I should have been more gracious."

"Yes, you should have."

Stacy sensed an underlying spirit of wry humor

in his otherwise derogatory comment and decided to play along. "You're not going to make this easy, are you?"

"Nope."

She thought she'd heard him chuckle. Because she couldn't be certain, she wasn't sure whether she ought to continue being so outspoken. "I am sorry, Gray. This conversation is getting us nowhere. I shouldn't have bothered you."

"That's right, you shouldn't have. But you did, so the way I see it, you owe me."

"Owe you what?" Her eyebrows knit.

"That dinner date you keep avoiding," he said smugly. "Just name the time."

Stacy felt trapped. "I can't. I'm on vacation and I intend to relax completely while I'm up here."

"Okay. How about next week?" He hesitated. "Oops. That won't work for me. I have other plans."

"Good," she said with relief. "You see? We aren't meant to be together for dinner." *Or any other time.*

Gray thought about keeping his plans from her, then changed his mind. Stacy might be able to offer valuable tips on how to approach Candace with regard to his taking Missy along when he volunteered at the camp. She might also have advice on dealing with the little girl if she suddenly decided she didn't want to behave.

Pressing Stacy to meet him for dinner, however, was clearly not going to work. If he wanted to speak with her, to ask her advice without putting her on the defensive or making her think he was trying to manipulate her, he'd better find another way.

He yawned noisily. "Okay. Apology accepted. Can I go back to sleep, now, or was there something else?"

"No. No, there's nothing else. Good night."

"Night."

The moment he hung up, Stacy felt strangely lonely. That was not a good sign. Neither was the fondness she'd noticed creeping into her tone, into her thoughts, as they'd talked.

Only one thing could be worse. She'd also sensed an affectionate quality to Gray's voice, even when he'd been teasing her. If he'd been getting the same impression of her as she had of him, they were both in trouble.

Stacy shivered and wrapped her arms around herself for comfort. It had been a long time since she'd missed someone the way she was missing Gray. It was as if he'd become an integral part of her life. Nothing could be farther from the truth.

Padding softly to the window, she looked up at the night sky, marveling at the clarity of the stars and the brightness of the waxing moon. In a few more days the moon would be full and the landscape would glow silver. Already the fireflies were blinking iridescent green and rising from the glens, making the oaks look as if they were festooned with Christmas lights.

Stacy sighed. Holidays were always hard on her. They brought back memories of her first ten years, of the happy childhood she'd spent with her parents. She'd never really gotten over losing them. Years had passed and she'd made a new life, but the deep sense of loss remained. So did her resolve to never allow anyone else to mean that much to her.

Surely, that couldn't be why she'd never gotten along with any of her foster parents. Or could it? Had the problem really been hers, alone?

Awed by the implications of her supposedly random thoughts, Stacy closed her eyes, stood very still and turned a willing heart toward her Heavenly Father.

She waited. Trusted Jesus completely. Just as she had when she'd first become a Christian. And she was rewarded. It didn't take a special prayer or a complicated ritual to bring her the peace she was seeking.

All it took was simple surrender.

Chapter Eleven

Gray arrived at the Spring River Campground late the following afternoon and parked in an empty camping spot. He'd had to shorten a couple of business appointments and postpone his four o'clock in order to give himself time to buy supplies. Hopefully, his crazy plan was worth the effort.

Rather than rely solely on Stacy's innate sense of fairness he'd decided on a lighthearted approach. Opening the trunk of the BMW he proceeded to set up a temporary camp, complete with a red-and-white checked tablecloth for the picnic table. Last, he reached into the ice chest for one plastic-wrapped package of hot dogs and picked up the long-handled barbecue tongs he'd just bought. Hamburgers would have been better but he wasn't sure how to cook them over an open fire, so he'd opted for the wieners.

With one last look around to convince himself everything was ready, he started up the hill, dinner in hand.

When he knocked on the door to Judy and Angie's cabin, Gray felt a surge of unaccustomed anxiety. Was he making a mistake by appealing to Stacy's sense of humor? Maybe he should just go back to the car, get his tie and his suit coat, and present himself in a more dignified manner. That was certainly the way he usually asked a woman to dine with him.

Lost in thought, he was startled when the cabin door was jerked open and he stood face-to-face with the lovely reason he'd gone to all this trouble. He didn't have to work at producing a silly grin. It spread across his face all by itself.

"Hi. I was in the neighborhood and thought I'd stop by." He held up the package of hot dogs and the tongs. "I brought dinner. With buns. And potato chips. And plastic plates with pictures of flowers on them. I hope that isn't too fancy for you."

She was taken aback. Gray looked utterly endearing, standing there with his shirtsleeves rolled up and no necktie. There was no way she could refuse him.

"Legendary tube steaks!" Stacy clapped her hands. "My favorite. How did you know?"

"It was a lucky guess," he said, relieved. "I was afraid to bring something like steak and have you think I was acting too upscale."

"Or find out I was a vegetarian after you'd spent all that money, like the client you told me about."

He wanted to assure her the money didn't matter, that spending time with her was all he really cared about, but he knew better than to reveal his true sentiments. Having them was bad enough. Confessing them would be idiotic. Considering the way Stacy felt about him and his family, he was lucky she hadn't slammed the door in his face when he'd showed up unannounced.

Gray nodded. "Right. So, are you hungry? My car's parked down the hill in one of the camping spots. I have the table loaded with goodies. All we have to do is light a fire and roast these." He displayed the plastic package.

"Okay. Give me a minute to brush my hair and grab my sandals."

"Sure. Fine." Waiting at the open door he watched Stacy hurry away. She was wearing jeans, as usual, and a pale-blue T-shirt. Nothing striking. Nothing chic. Yet every time he saw her she looked prettier. There was a wholesome appeal about her that made him wish they didn't live such dissimilar lives and weren't so unsuited to each other.

Disturbing thoughts like those had been popping into Gray's head for weeks. It was getting harder and harder to dismiss them. Instead, he sought to reason through the situation. Although he and Stacy were both Christians, that was where their similarity ended. The only other thing they had in common was a fondness for Missy.

He chuckled to himself. And one more thing: relationship difficulties with his parents—Nathan, in particular. Sighing, he shook his head. Short of moving to the opposite side of the globe and changing his name, there was no way he'd ever be unhampered by his family. Like it or not, they were a part of him, of his life. Especially his mother. Now that he knew what she'd done, what she'd put up with all those years for his sake, he could never turn his back on her. And she and Nathan were a package deal. Accept one and you got both.

Stacy returned and caught him brooding. "Hey. If you've changed your mind about cooking my dinner, say so. I can always eat here with Judy and Angie."

"No, no. I'm sorry. I was just thinking."

"Well, cut it out. You look like your best friend just disowned you."

"On the contrary." Gray's smile returned. "As a matter of fact, I'd like to tell you about my best friend. James and I roomed together in college. He's the one who led me to the Lord. I'll be working with him next week, which is why I wasn't free to have dinner with you then." Gray gestured toward the path leading to his campsite. "Come on. I'll tell you all about it while we eat."

The blaze he built in the fire ring quickly grew so hot Stacy had to move back. "Whew! I think that's big enough," she said, fanning herself with an extra paper plate.

Gray stopped before adding the last of the precut bundle of wood he'd bought when he'd picked up the camping supplies. When he straightened, the thick smoke seemed to follow him and he waved it away. "Okay. Whatever you say. I've never built a campfire before."

"No kidding?" She tried not to laugh at his efforts. "You could have fooled me."

"Yeah. I'll bet." Joining her on the picnic bench farthest from the flames, he grinned knowingly. "I'm beginning to see that primitive skills aren't as simple as they look."

"You really haven't ever been camping? Not even as a little boy? How sad."

"You've met my parents. What do you think?"

Stacy chose to tease him rather than comment negatively about his family. "I think…you should have brought your butler along to look after you."

Gray shook his head. "Don't have one. Never saw the need. I do have a cook, as I said before, but other than that I take care of myself. Except for the woman who comes in twice a week to clean and do the laundry, of course."

"Oh, I see. You rough it." Stacy cast a wry smile in his direction. "How challenging that must be."

"I manage." Innocently reaching for her hand, Gray suddenly realized what he was about to do and stopped himself just in time. "So, did you go camping a lot when you were a kid?"

"Not often. It depended on which foster family I happened to be living with. Most of the outdoor lore I've learned came from taking tracking and survival courses." Reflecting on his lack of skill in the woods, she smiled more broadly. "It wouldn't hurt you to study the subject a little, too. With Missy for a niece, you may find you need the expertise."

Gray raked his fingers through his hair. "I know. It's scary to think of how close we came to losing her the first time she ran off." When the urge struck this time, he allowed himself to act. He grasped Stacy's fingers, cradled them in one hand and covered them gently with the other. "I'll never be able to thank you enough."

Rather than let herself think about how wonderful his touch was or how much she wanted it to continue, she chose to treat the intimate moment lightly. "Like I told your assistant when she called, I expect my fee to be paid in Gummi Bears." The resulting grin on Gray's face warmed her far more than the fire.

"You do? I guess she forgot to tell me."

"I don't doubt it. That woman sounded way too professional to take me seriously."

He continued to hold Stacy's hand. "I hope I never make the same mistake."

Their conversation was getting too serious. Stacy pulled away and got to her feet. The only mistake *she'd* made was agreeing to have anything more to do with Graydon Payne. Her thoughts about him were already too tender, too intimate, to be rational. The more time she spent with him, the greater the risk she might forget her place; might convince herself to overlook the danger inherent in falling in love with a man like Gray. *With Gray.*

Stacy caught her breath. A tremor of awareness came alive in her soul. Softhearted idiot that she was, she'd fallen head over heels in love with the one man who was everything she'd always sworn she'd avoid! Now what? she asked herself.

The answer came easily. *Now nothing.* Graydon Payne was never going to learn how she felt about him. The problem was hers. She didn't intend to add embarrassment to her list of blunders.

The safest thing to do was to change the subject, so she said, "Speaking of serious, when do we eat? I'm starving."

"It beats me. Maybe we can find a Boy Scout around here who can tell us when the fire's ready."

"That won't be necessary. It looks like it's died down enough to keep from incinerating us or our dinner. Where did you put the sticks?"

"What sticks?" Gray's brow knit.

"The sticks we roast the hot dogs on."

"Oops."

Stacy stared at him. "Are you sure you're the same genius who makes his fortune arranging successful, multimillion-dollar partnerships?" Incredulous, she shook her head. "Hard to believe."

"I am not required to roast wieners in the course of my job," Gray countered. "When I'm entertaining clients or planning a big launch party for one of my projects, I have the affair catered. Besides, I brought tongs." He brandished them. "Won't these do?"

"Sure. You grab a hot dog, hold it over the fire and let me know when those short, metal handles get too hot to touch. In the meantime, I'll open the mustard and get the buns ready."

Gray was not going to give up. "Okay. Then we'll use twigs from the trees. That should work."

"Well…" She began to laugh softly. "You can do that if you want to but count me out. By the time you get the food hot, you'll probably have burned through the wood and dumped your whole project into the hot coals. I prefer my tube steaks *not* coated with ashes and grit, let alone tree bark."

"Okay, smartie. Just what do you suggest?"

"A raid on Judy's closets for wire hangers. Preferably ones without a plastic coating." Stacy started up the hill toward the cabin and called back, "Wait there. I'll find something we can use."

I could use fresh start, Gray thought, shaking his head in self-derision. All his plans had been carefully contrived and executed. All his purchases had been designed to impress Stacy with his ability to adapt to her idea of fun. And because he'd neglected to bring metal rods to spear a stupid hot dog, she was laughing at his incompetence instead of praising his know-how.

He'd wanted to impress her. All he'd done was prove how inept he was at doing so.

Judy caught Stacy pulling a blouse from her closet, slipping it off the hanger and dropping it into a heap on the bed. "Hey!"

Startled, she jumped back, her cheeks burning. "Oh! You scared me."

"Good. I just ironed that blouse."

Still a little breathless, Stacy said, "Oh, you did not. You don't iron any more than I do. If it weren't for permanent press we'd both be so wrinkled people would think we'd slept in our clothes." She laughed nervously. "Which, come to think of it, I've done more than once when I've been stuck all night in the woods."

"Okay. So maybe I did exaggerate. I still want to know what you're doing."

"Um..." Stacy held up the hanger. "I need some wiener-roasting sticks."

"Why? We're having lasagna for dinner."

"I'm not," Stacy admitted. Her blush heightened to make her cheeks even rosier. "I'm having a picnic...in the campground...with Gray."

"Oooh! When did you change your mind about him?"

"I haven't changed my mind. I'm simply taking your good advice and being kind. He came to the door and—"

"And you couldn't send him away?" Judy cheered, fist in the air, "All right!"

"It's just a simple picnic, okay? Don't go blowing it up into anything more." Stacy pulled a face. "I think he brought marshmallows, too. Can I have two hangers so we don't have to share?"

"I shouldn't give you another one," Judy said with a knowing smile. "Two on a marshmallow is kind of fun. If the other person is your type, that is."

"Well, Graydon Payne isn't mine," Stacy insisted. She fell back on wisecracking to keep from facing the seriousness of her upcoming time alone with Gray. "And I'm not sharing with him, so fork over some usable wire, lady, or suffer the consequences."

Judy reached into the closet, came up with an empty hanger and handed it to Stacy. "Here. Enjoy."

"I knew you'd see the wisdom of cooperation."

"Hah," Judy said. "It's a good thing one of us has a little wisdom left to share. You seem to be fresh out."

"Meaning?"

"Meaning, the man has been making himself a part of your life ever since he saw you again. How many times does he have to show up before you realize that he's courting you?"

"He is not!" Stacy faced her friend, hands on her hips, eyes wide.

"Have it your way." Judy shrugged and started out of the room. "Come on. I'll get you a wire cutter. You need to get back to Gray before he comes looking for you and I make a pass at him myself.''

''If you're trying to make me jealous, it isn't working,'' Stacy insisted.

''Jealous? Me make you jealous?'' Judy laughed heartily. ''Why, whatever gave you that idea?''

Gray couldn't help fidgeting. Out of his element, he wondered what other faux pas he'd commit before the evening was over. When he saw Stacy coming back down the hill he forced himself to feign nonchalance.

''Got them,'' she called, waving the wires.

''Good. I think the fire's still hot enough.''

She agreed. ''As big as it was, it'll be hours before the embers cool off.'' Handing him one of the wires, she threaded a hot dog on hers and held it over the fire, trying to ignore Gray as he followed suit. Judy couldn't have been right about his motives, could she? Was it possible he'd engineered their prior meetings?

The ridiculous idea was dismissed as soon as Stacy analyzed it. He certainly hadn't caused Missy to run away or to get stuck in the little storage closet. Beyond that, all he'd been doing was asking advice on how to deal with the child, or trying to pay his emotional debt to search and rescue. There was certainly nothing romantic about that. Then again, he had set up a picnic, which was totally out of character for him.

Stacy twirled the wire to roast her hot dog

evenly. When Gray crouched down beside her and his presence made her pulse speed, she decided the safest thing to do was to focus on the lonely child. "So, how's Missy doing these days?"

"That's why I came to see you," he said.

Though she should have been happy to hear it, Stacy had to admit she was more disappointed than relieved. "Is there a problem?"

"Not exactly. I just have a question for you." He stared into the fire. "I'm volunteering as a counselor at a children's church camp, up in Ravenden, next week."

"I know the place. It's very nice."

"Glad to hear it. So, what do you think about my enrolling Missy and taking her with me?"

"Does she want to go?"

"I haven't asked her yet. I thought I should speak with Candace and Mark about it first, in case they refuse to allow her to go. I didn't want to promise anything I couldn't deliver."

"That's wise," Stacy said. "Missy's a bright little girl but she's still a kid. Kids don't think the same way you and I do. To them, everything tends to be equal."

"For instance?"

"Oh, like the promise of an ice cream cone or a pony. We don't see those things as being of the same importance. To a child, they are. To them, a promise is a promise. It's far better to avoid making one in the first place than to offer something you can't deliver." She sensed him turn his head, begin to study her profile.

Afraid that her expression might betray too much of what was in her heart, Stacy stood up. "Well, time to grab a hot dog bun and see if my cooking is as good as I think it is."

"I'm sure it is," Gray said. "There's nothing you don't do well."

Her laugh was nervous, cynical. "Oh, yes there is."

"Okay. What?" He joined her at the picnic table.

Stacy scooted around the end of the table and chose a place directly across from him rather than give him another opportunity to hold her hand. Not that she hadn't enjoyed his touch. She was avoiding him because she'd liked it *too* much.

Spreading mustard and relish to stall for time while she composed herself, Stacy finally passed the plastic containers to Gray and dared to meet his gaze. "I can't tell you my faults. If I did, you wouldn't think I was perfect anymore."

When Gray smiled over at her and said, "Yes, I would," the sincere look in his eyes was almost enough to bring her to tears.

It was dusk before Stacy convinced herself to end the picnic. "I guess I should be going."

Gray put out his hand but didn't touch her. "No. Wait. We haven't roasted marshmallows yet."

"Really, I..." Pausing, she realized she wanted

to stay with him. Forever. Their evening together had been the most enjoyable time she could remember ever having. Her initial nervousness had been replaced with a tranquil accord that had arrived with such subtlety that she hadn't sensed it coming until it had already filled her soul to overflowing.

"Stay a while longer. Your friends will understand. Come on. Show me how this is done." He reached for the bag of marshmallows and tore it open.

"As if you couldn't figure it out by yourself." She popped a plain marshmallow into her mouth. "I like them better uncooked, anyway." Gray's lopsided smile of response made her wish he wasn't so blasted endearing.

"I'll bet there's a special technique to roasting them. I need to learn what it is so I don't disappoint Missy or the other kids when I help out at camp."

"You're really going to do that?"

"Sure. Why not?"

Stacy stifled a giggle. "No reason. Just make sure you don't sign up to demonstrate forest lore to them, okay? You owe the poor, innocent kids that much."

"I beg your pardon?" Pantomiming a terrible affront, he clapped a hand over his heart. "Are you suggesting that I might not be the best person to teach young minds about the wonders of nature?"

This time, Stacy laughed aloud. "I'm not *sug-*

gesting anything. I'm telling you. Do everybody a favor and stick to civilization. That's where you belong.''

He threaded a stack of three marshmallows on his makeshift skewer and held it over a remaining spot of glowing coals. ''Only because you refuse to teach me all you know.''

''Oh, right! Like I could do that in a couple of hours?'' Too late, she realized he'd been goading her again so she added, ''And if you claim I know so little you can learn it that fast, I'm going to conk you with a marshmallow.''

''Sure, you are.'' Forgetting his task, he concentrated on enjoying the verbal sparring with Stacy. Nothing got past her, did it? She was one of a kind, always ready to stand up to him, to give as good as she got.

Still feigning insult and racking her brain for a quick-witted comeback, she glanced at the end of his hanger. It was in flames. ''Um, excuse me, Mr. Payne, but I believe your dessert is on fire.''

''What?'' Gray jerked the stick back and blew hard on the bubbling, blackened mess to quell the flames. Part of the melting confection started to slide off. He caught it without thinking. ''Ouch!''

''Well, silly…'' Stacy began before she realized the sticky, clinging sweet could actually be hurting him. She jumped to her feet. ''Let go. Drop it.''

By the time he did as he was told, his palm was red beneath the goo. Stacy quickly led him to the cooler, scooped up some cracked ice and filled his hand, closing his fingers by placing her smaller hands over his. "Here. Hold on to this. It'll stop the burning. I can't believe you did that."

"Neither can I." Gray stared at their joined hands. He marveled at the expert way she had reacted to help him. He hadn't meant to do something so idiotic, but if he'd known Stacy was going to minister to him so tenderly, he'd have grabbed the burning marshmallow on purpose.

Dazed by the effect their personal contact was having on her, she abruptly loosened her grip, stepped back, and took refuge in becoming fully professional once again. "I suspect it's only a first or second-degree burn. If it blisters or the skin breaks for any reason, be sure to keep it clean, dry and sterile. If you notice any reddening later or if the pain worsens, I suggest you see a doctor."

"I will."

His voice was restrained, his expression unreadable, giving Stacy no clue as to his feelings. She was having no problem discerning her own emotions, though. For the few moments when she'd forgotten herself and cupped Gray's injured hand, she'd been filled with an indescribable sensation of pure wonder.

Seeking to distract them both, she decided to demonstrate the proper marshmallow-roasting technique. "Here. Watch me. You string the marshmallow on the skewer like this, the same way you did, only you hold it farther away from the heat. Turn it often enough to keep it from catching on fire. It should be a toasty-brown color...not black.'' She crouched down and slowly twirled her wire over the glowing embers. ''When it starts to bubble under the crust, it's done.''

Stacy had been concentrating on her task rather than letting herself think about Gray. Now, she stood and proudly presented the perfectly roasted marshmallow, taking pains to avoid making eye contact with him. ''See? It's easy when you pay attention.'' He didn't reply.

Still jittery and far more aware of him than she liked, Stacy listened to the warnings blaring in her brain and offered the polite excuse, ''Well, I guess I'd better be going. Judy will be expecting me back and Angie's probably made dessert, again, and—'' Stop babbling and just go, she ordered silently.

Gray's voice was quiet, compelling. ''Aren't you going to give me a taste of that?''

''Oh, sure. No problem.'' Without thinking, she carefully slid the sticky, half-melted confection off the wire and held it up. ''Here you go.''

She'd expected him to reach for it, to take it in his free hand. Instead, he stepped closer, leaned over, and opened his mouth. When she looked up into his eyes, she saw a well-defined challenge. One she couldn't refuse.

Unfortunately, when she tried to pop the marshmallow into his mouth without touching him, it stuck to her.

Gray's mouth closed over the treat, his lips warmly, gently, grazing the tips of her fingers. Her eyes widened. Her heart stopped. The challenge in his dark eyes became a caress; the mutual sharing of an intimate moment that stole her breath away.

She withdrew her tingling fingers as she watched him lick his lips. Lips that had once kissed her.

But only as a joke, Stacy insisted, trying to counteract her amorous reaction to him the way she had before. This time, it didn't help. The atmosphere between her and Gray had become so charged with emotional intensity Stacy couldn't even bring herself to look away, let alone convince herself that he wasn't serious.

Gray was momentarily stunned. He studied her face, her eyes, trying to see into her heart and decide if she was feeling as off balance as he was.

It was impossible to tell. Stacy looked as if she were torn between fondness and fright. Did she think he'd ever hurt her? Cause her pain? He'd *never* do such a thing. Except that he already had, he admitted ruefully. When he'd taken it upon himself to interfere in her relationship with Mark, he'd undoubtedly hurt her terribly. No wonder she still distrusted him.

Concerned only for Stacy, Gray purposely broke the mood and released her by saying, "Thanks for the taste. I'll be sure and remember your recipe." He backed away. "When you get back to the cabin, tell Judy and Angie hello for me."

"I—I will." She saw him start to stick both hands in his pockets, then flinch when the burned one touched fabric. "You take care of your hand. Remember what I said."

"I will."

Stacy was sidestepping toward the edge of the campsite. "And tell Missy I said she should behave while she's at camp, even if you're there, too." She saw him nod. Then he turned away. Stacy did the same and headed for the cabin.

She felt as drained as if she'd just run a marathon. What was the matter with her? Didn't she have any good sense left? If Gray hadn't acted first, she doubted she'd have been able to muster enough self-control to walk away from him. And *then* what?

Stacy didn't want to know. She didn't even want to guess. If, as she suspected, the Lord was trying to make another point with her in regard to her feelings toward Graydon Payne, she'd just as soon fail to grasp it.

How long God would let her get away with that attitude was another question altogether.

Chapter Twelve

Missy had jumped up and down with glee when Gray had informed her he was taking her to camp with him. The only thing she'd objected to was having to share a cabin with ten other girls and their twenty-something female counselor, Miss Emily, instead of becoming her uncle's shadow.

On the fourth day of the five scheduled, the child finally quit sulking and began to act as if she were having a good time. Her group was seated in the shade of a cluster of ancient oaks, making animals out of pinecones, when Gray sauntered up and joined them.

"Look, Uncle Gray! I made a owl. Miss Emily showed me how. See?" Missy displayed it proudly, waiting for his admiration.

He smiled down at the eager child. "That's very pretty, honey."

"I wanted to make a dog like Lewis, but it was too hard." She began to pout, then brightened. "When are you going to take me to see his puppies?"

Gray had forgotten all about the pups at Stacy's. After the incident of the hot marshmallows and equally heated ambience, he figured she'd never want to hear from him again, let alone have him show up on her doorstep.

"I didn't say we'd go see the puppies, Missy. That was your idea. Remember?"

"Stacy said I could."

"Well, she shouldn't have." Frustrated, he raked his fingers through his hair.

"But—but I asked Jesus, too," Missy insisted.

If only things were actually as simple as the trusting heart of a child saw them. Searching for a way to appease her, Gray said, "Tell you what. I'll talk to Mark and Candace and see if it's okay to take you to the zoo next week. Then you can see lots of different animals. Okay?"

When Missy didn't answer right away he waited, expecting tears. Surprisingly, she didn't cry or pout. Instead, she stared up at him, eyes wide, expression incredulous, as if he'd just grown a second head.

"Okay?" he asked again.

Without answering, the little girl lowered her gaze and went back to adding more make-believe feathers to her owl.

* * *

At dinner that evening, Missy's counselor, Emily, approached Gray's table. "Hi. Did you two have fun, today?"

Confused, he looked up at the dark-haired, amiable young woman. "Pardon me?"

"You and Missy," she explained. "I only let her go because you said she could."

He was on his feet in an instant, his meal forgotten. "You let her go? Where?"

"To meet you." Emily squinted up at him. "You did tell her she could. I heard you talking to her and I'm sure you promised to take her to see some animals."

"At the zoo. Not *today*." The hair on the back of his neck was bristling. Running away from his mother's house or disappearing at Stacy's was one thing. Getting lost in the wilderness, like the first time she ran away, was quite another. "I haven't seen Missy since I visited your group and saw her making an owl."

"Oh, dear." Emily's eyes widened in fear and disbelief. "Why would she lie to me like that?"

"I'm afraid she has a one-track mind when it comes to some subjects, especially a certain rescue dog." Angry, Gray couldn't make up his mind who to be mad at first: himself, Emily, Stacy or God. He fought the urge to run out of the dining hall and shout the little girl's name at the top of his lungs, even though he knew it probably wouldn't help.

Emily was wringing her hands. Tears were starting to trickle down her cheeks. "What are we going to do?"

"I don't want you to worry," Gray said, lightly patting her shoulder to comfort her. "Sit down, eat your dinner and look after the rest of your group. I'll tell James what's going on. I know what Missy is expecting, and that's exactly what I'm going to do."

Stacy's emergency beeper went off as she was coming out of the grocery store in Cave City. She directed the clerk's helper to her truck so he could load her purchases in the back, then went to a pay phone to call her message service.

"This is Stacy Lucas. What do you have for me?"

"A lost child," the operator said. "A six-year-old girl. I wasn't sure if I should bother you. The call didn't come from any of your regular sources but the man said it was urgent. He sure sounded like he meant it."

Stacy's stomach leaped into her throat and stuck there like a big wad of dry cotton. "What was his name?"

"He said it was Payne. I didn't catch his first name. It was real unusual, though."

Not again! "Could his name have been Graydon Payne?"

"Might have been. Hard to say. He was talking so fast I could hardly understand a word he said."

Suddenly light-headed, Stacy leaned against the

edge of the wall-mounted phone booth. She and Gray had gotten used to chasing after Missy. If he was upset, the current situation must be serious. "Where was the child last seen?"

"At a camp up in…" Shuffling papers, the operator found her notes. "In Ravenden. Is that too far away for you? I can always call somebody else if you'd like."

"No," Stacy said quickly. "I know exactly where it is. It's not too far."

"You sure? This guy sounded kind of dithered."

"I don't doubt that a bit." Stacy was already laying out her route in her head and going over the supplies she'd need. "Call Mr. Payne back and tell him I'll try to be there in about an hour. And tell him not to worry. I'll be bringing Lewis."

"I thought you'd decided to retire that dog?"

"I had. But this is a special case. Lewis already knows the missing child so he's the best choice."

"I suppose that's why the guy asked for you by name."

"Undoubtedly," Stacy said flatly. "I'll be on the road in five minutes. Bye."

She'd hung up and was running for her truck before the operator had a chance to respond.

The idea of seeing Gray again was so physically unsettling and had built to such a peak by the time she reached Ravenden, Stacy wondered if she might be coming down with the flu.

"I should be so lucky," she muttered. Beside her, Lewis thumped his tail. "Yeah, I know. You love this."

Uptight beyond belief, she made a disgusted face. There it was again—the *L* word! What a mockery her indiscriminate, unconscious thoughts had made of her determination to put Gray out of her mind for good.

"Yeah, yeah, go ahead and wag your tail, Lewis." Stacy gave him a pat of assurance to counteract her slightly gruff tone. "At least one of us is going to have fun tonight. But it sure isn't going to be me."

Scowling, she wheeled into the hard-packed dirt drive leading to the children's summer camp. The place had been there so long and had such a sterling reputation, it was always full to capacity. And no wonder. The kids were well-fed, entertained, and housed in dormlike buildings with real beds instead of having to pitch tents on the hard ground. As far as Stacy was concerned, that was *not* camping.

Gray was pacing and waiting for her at the archway marking the main entrance. When she stopped beside him, he reached for the door handle on the passenger side of her truck, spotted Lewis, and changed his mind.

"I'll just ride back here, instead," he said, vaulting over the side of the truck bed with ease.

Stacy opened the sliding window behind her so they could still communicate and called, "Move over here so we can talk. You can fill me in while I drive. Where should we start?''

"Past the main campground and then to the east," he said, hanging on to the window frame for balance and crouching behind her. "That's where I last saw Missy."

Other children were grouped around the dining hall doorway, watching the truck pass, so Stacy slowed down. Looking in the rearview mirror she saw Gray gesturing.

"Turn there, at the rail fence," he ordered. "It's not a regular road but it's passable almost all the way. We can save time if we drive."

Stacy didn't park until the trail got too narrow for her truck to squeeze through. Lewis was straining at his leash, eager to begin, the moment she got out of the truck.

"Hand me my backpack before you climb down," she told Gray. "Everything slid around back there on that crooked stretch of road between here and Hardy."

Gray complied, then joined her. He held up the pack so she could slip her arms through the shoulder straps. "No kidding. Do you always stir your groceries like that?"

"Not hardly." She glanced at the dimly lit disarray in the truck bed. The day was nearly over. Long shadows from the trees blurred her jumbled cargo even more. "Grab a couple of bottles of water, if you can find them in all that mess, and something sweet, too, for energy."

"Right. What else?"

Stacy assessed his clothing. Jeans, hiking boots, a T-shirt and windbreaker were better choices than he'd made the last time they'd hit the trail together. "That's all. You'll do just as you are. Stuff the extra provisions in your jacket pockets and let's go."

He followed her orders without hesitation, then led the way to the glen where Missy was last seen. "Her group was sitting over there, under those trees, making animals out of pinecones. She started talking about Lewis. Said she wanted to go see his puppies. Like a fool I didn't realize how important it was to her."

"It's not your fault," Stacy said. "Missy has to be held responsible for her own actions someday. If something bothered her, she should have spoken up, come to you and told you how she was feeling. Unless she learns to do that she's never going to be able to cope with the changes in life that she *can't* control."

He wanted to say, "I think she left so you'd come after her," but decided to keep that opinion to himself. It wasn't fair to attribute his personal wishes to Missy. Maybe her wanting to see Stacy again had nothing to do with what had happened. Maybe the little girl was merely so spoiled, so used to getting her own way, she'd disappeared to punish him when he'd refused her request to go see the pups.

"I really thought she liked me, trusted me,"

Gray said, clearly sorrowing. He sighed. "I guess I was wrong."

The pathos in his voice cut all the way to Stacy's soul and made its home there. How such a caring, sensitive man could have come from the Payne clan, could have developed in the same family that had shaped Mark and the others, was a complete mystery to her.

To say so, however, would be a really stupid move. Assuming she was able to compliment Gray without sounding overly judgmental about the others, he could still misunderstand her motives. He might even think she was making a pass at him! Then what? The compelling possibilities of such a scenario sent her imagination into overdrive, making her blush. *Oh, heavens.*

"Heaven, indeed," Stacy muttered, disgusted with her wandering mind. "I think you and I should pray hard that everything works out tonight."

"I've already been praying nonstop."

She made a disgusted face. "Well, I hate to admit it, but I haven't. That's a bad habit of mine. I tend to wait till things are about as bad as they can get before I panic and ask God for help."

Closing her eyes and bowing her head she said, "Father, it's me again. Late, as usual. Please help us find Missy and keep her safe while we search."

Gray was about to add his *Amen* when Stacy went on, "And thank you for giving her an uncle who loves her and cares what happens to her, no matter how she behaves.''

It suddenly struck her how the same kind of tolerance was available from God when any person became his child. And in *her* case, it was sure a good thing He allowed mistakes. Boy, was it!

Continuing in silent prayer for a few moments, Stacy finally said, ''Amen.'' When she lifted her gaze to meet Gray's she saw a sparkle of unshed tears in his eyes. That was no real surprise. She'd known for some time that her former nemesis had a tender heart.

Which merely meant he was living the Christian life as well as he could, with God's help. It did not, however, mean he'd renounced the trappings of his elaborate life-style or was any closer to understanding why different kinds of things were more important to her.

Stacy knew that critical truth had better be foremost in her befuddled brain or she'd be prone to add another bad blunder to her already considerable list of them. It would be far too easy to heed her secret yearnings and make the mistake of thinking Gray cared as much about her as she did about him. Maybe even returned her love!

Her heart skipped a beat. Allowing herself to imagine something like that, to dwell on it, would be the crowning disaster in a life already jam-packed with them. To love, with no chance of receiving equal love in return, was not only foolish, it was pointless. She'd been brought there for only one thing. To save lives.

This time, Stacy remembered to ask for help before she was in dire straits. *Father,* she called silently, *please help me keep my mind on my job and my heart focused on what you've put me here for.*

Instantly, her concentration peaked and she was back on track. "Come on, Lewis," she said with eagerness and confidence. "Let's go. We've got work to do."

Guiding the dog to the tree Gray had indicated, she ordered, "Find Missy."

The ridge they mounted was topped with a thick growth of small oaks and sycamores, interspersed with a smattering of cedars and an occasional green briar. Gray had learned to avoid the wiry, thorny vines the hard way, by grabbing one.

He drew up beside Stacy, breathing hard, and switched off the flashlight she'd given him. The batteries wouldn't last if they used the lights too much. "Well? What do you think?"

Stacy had been watching the sky, noting recent changes. Some stars still shone through the clouds but thunderheads were building, darkening. She didn't like the humid feel of the air or the lingering heat, either. If the dew point was as high as she figured it was, they could be in for some rotten weather.

"I think we'd better find Missy pretty soon or we're all going to get very wet," she said flatly.

"Look at those clouds. I can feel a change coming."

"I was thinking the same thing. I'd hoped it was just my imagination."

"I hope so, too, but I doubt it. See how antsy Lewis is? He knows something's up."

Gray nodded. "Maybe we're close to finding Missy."

"Maybe. How does she cope in thunderstorms? Do they scare her?" Worried, Stacy let Lewis lead her down the opposite side of the ridge with Gray following close behind.

"I don't know. I hope not. We—I mean Mark and Candace—haven't had her that long."

"I was afraid of that. I just hope she doesn't take shelter under a big tree when the lightning starts. That's the worst thing she can do."

"One of the counselors mentioned that kind of danger the first day we were up here," Gray said. "Assuming Missy listened. She was still mad at me for making her bunk with all the other girls."

"I imagine she was. I can see how emotionally attached to you she is. It's too bad…" Thunder drowned her out.

"What did you say?"

Stacy shook her head, disgusted with the fanciful idea she'd almost expressed. Missy didn't need a man like Gray. She needed a real home, with two parents to love her, not a bachelor father whose absence would constantly remind her of the daddy she'd lost. Missy's real daddy had tried to raise his child alone and look what had happened.

"Nothing. I was just rambling," Stacy hedged. "Now be quiet and let me concentrate on doing my job, okay?"

"Sure. Sorry."

"I'm the one who should apologize. I'm just jumpy tonight."

"Join the club."

"I'm afraid I'm already a charter member." She pressed her lips into a thin line, more determined than ever to find Missy for him. "I'm going to let Lewis go as fast as he wants from now on. It'll be dangerous going up and down these hills at that pace, especially in the dark, so if you want to drop back, I'll understand."

"You've got to be kidding. I'm sticking to you and that dog like glue."

Pleased, she said, "Good. Watch your step, then, and don't crowd me. Here we go."

Chapter Thirteen

The rumble of thunder echoed across the green hills like the constant beat of faraway drums. Incessant lightning reflected off the heavy clouds to illuminate the entire sky and forest below. The still, humid air was charged with electricity.

"I don't like the feel of this," Stacy called back.

Gray studied the horizon through the trees. "I agree. Look at that cloud wall."

Stacy knew exactly what he meant. She'd been watching the almost straight black line of the weather front as it developed. It lay suspended above the lighter horizon like a menacing blanket. If a tornado developed, they'd probably spot it in that eerie glow beneath the cloud line.

She pulled Lewis to a stop, wiped perspiration from her forehead, and said, "Whew. This is a workout. You holding up okay?"

"I'm fine." Leaning over, Gray rested his hands on his knees and took full advantage of the brief time-out. "Why are we stopping? Is something wrong?"

"No. Just taking a breather." Stacy pointed. "Look how green the sky is."

"I noticed. What do you think we should do?"

"Well, quitting is out of the question," she answered immediately. "And I don't suppose you'd consider going back for your own safety and letting Lewis and me find Missy by ourselves."

"Not a chance."

"I didn't think so." She smiled at him. "You do have your good points, Mr. Payne."

"I hope so. Do you think we're getting close?"

"We have to be. An adult, walking at normal speed, can travel about two miles in an hour. That equals a twelve-square mile search area, which multiplies to fifty square miles the second hour. But Missy's a child. She won't have made such good time." Pausing, Stacy patted her dog. "And we have Lewis, which definitely throws the odds into our favor. We'll find her."

"I sure hope you're right." Gray eyed the cloud wall. "At this point, I wouldn't even mind some wind or rain."

"I know what you mean. Anything to break up the front. As soon as I give Lewis a drink we'll get going again." Making a shallow cup of one hand, she poured water into it from her canteen and offered it to the panting dog. "He shouldn't drink too much till we're done because he's working so hard, but this will give him some relief."

"How about you? Need more?" Gray asked, holding up one of the plastic bottles he'd gotten from her truck.

"I'm fine. You drink that," Stacy said. "Just don't overdo. I don't want to have to stop to doctor you."

"You won't." Gray tipped the bottle up and drank deeply. "I used to jog a lot when I was in college. Even ran a couple of marathons." He smiled wryly. "Don't ask me where I finished."

"Finishing at all is quite an accomplishment."

"Thanks." He tucked the small, half-empty bottle back into his pocket. "You ready?"

A bolt of lightning shot to earth over the next ridge, followed closely by an echoing boom of thunder that seemed to come from all around them. "I sure am. Let's go. I want us out of here as soon as possible!"

Lewis sailed over a low ridge, hesitated, sniffed the air, then leaped a huge, fallen tree and began to wiggle as if he'd just located his best buddy. He dodged back and forth so much in his excitement that his long leash tangled around some of the tree's broken limbs.

Squealing with glee, Missy threw her thin arms around the dog and kissed him. "Lewis! I knew you'd find me."

Gray scooped the little girl up in his arms before

Stacy could untangle her dog enough to properly restrain him. To her surprise, Lewis didn't bare his teeth this time.

"Missy, you have *got* to stop doing this. You're giving me hair to match my name." Gray's voice was gruff but his enormous relief was still evident.

The child didn't reply. She simply held tight to her uncle's neck and grinned at Stacy over his shoulder.

Greater thunder shook the trees. Flashes of lightning made the sky glow and flicker as if the clouds hid a thousand gigantic searchlights gone berserk.

"We need to find shelter," Stacy shouted above the din. "This weather is going to get real nasty in a few minutes."

"I know." Gray's arms were wrapped around the child, sheltering her as best he could. "What we need is a storm cellar. Or a cave."

"Fine. Where do you suggest we find one?"

Missy raised a thin arm and pointed. "Over there."

Stacy swung the beam of her flashlight and spotted a dark recess less than thirty feet away. It might be full of wild things that objected to sharing their haven, but it sure beat standing out in the open where they were prey to lightning, rain and hail. Not to mention the tornados this kind of erratic weather spawned.

She circled the fallen tree. Lewis's leash was hopelessly tangled. There was no time to waste trying to free it, so she released him, leaving it behind.

Her flashlight cut a hazy path through the damp atmosphere. "Missy's right. It is a cave! Come on."

Gray followed, carrying the little girl. "How do you know it's safe?"

"I don't," Stacy called back. "You're welcome to stay out here if you want." As if to punctuate her remarks, a few bits of hail the size of marbles began to strike the oak canopy overhead.

In seconds, the trees were being pummeled fiercely. Hail stung like a thousand needles when it struck Gray's shoulders and back. He bent over Missy, absorbing the battering to protect her, and made a run for it.

Stacy ducked into the limestone cave without pausing to assess its suitability. Gray was only a few seconds behind her. Lewis sniffed the ground and air while his mistress gathered everyone together in the widest spot by the door and started to give orders.

"Okay. We're safe enough for now. Wait here while I check out the rest of this place."

Gray reached out and grabbed her arm. "No. I'll do it. You stay here and take care of Missy." He lowered the clinging child to the ground at his feet.

"Oh, fine," Stacy said cynically. "And what can you do that I can't? Suppose you find a bear or something?"

Not about to let her deter him, he responded

with equal sarcasm. "Then it'll eat me and you two can run for it while I provide a distraction."

Missy squealed, "No!" and flung herself at his legs, gripping them at the knees.

Gray spoke soothingly to the frightened little girl. "We'll all be fine, honey. There aren't any bears. Honest."

Glancing at Stacy he saw her give a noncommittal shrug and start shining her flashlight on the cave floor in a back and forth pattern. If there was any danger she'd soon find it. He'd been behaving like a macho idiot to insist he should be the one to check the shallow cave when she was far more qualified to do so. The trouble was, he'd felt an overwhelming urge to protect her and had spoken up before considering the situation intellectually.

"I think we're fine," Stacy finally said. "If there were any large animals in here with us, Lewis would know it long before we did, anyway. Since he's settled right down, I have to assume he isn't worried, so I'm not, either." She shone her light on the spot where the dog lay. "See?"

Missy cooed, "Oh, poor Lewis," forgot everything else, and headed straight for the weary animal. Settling herself beside him she stroked him gently from head to tail. "I'm sorry I made you go out in the rain and get all tired."

Gray's cynical expression made Stacy chuckle and ask, "Hey, Missy, what about your uncle and me? We were *with* Lewis, you know."

Acting unusually shy, the little girl ducked her

head and curled up, half on and half off the gentle old dog.

"Give it up," Gray said dryly. "When it comes to a popularity contest between us and that dog, we both know who's going to win."

"With Missy, in particular," Stacy agreed. Now that their temporary crisis was over and they were sheltered from the elements, she wasn't sure what to do with herself. Or with Graydon Payne. The physical strain of the frenzied search was beginning to tell, though. The way she saw it, she could either stand there staring at him or sit down before she fell down.

She chose the latter, easing down right where she was. "I don't know about you, but I'm beat."

He shone his flashlight over the bare ground around her. "You sure it's safe to sit there?"

"Well, there aren't any snakes, scorpions or centipedes. I checked. So I guess so." Stacy yawned.

"Good. Then I'll join you."

Oops. That wasn't exactly what she'd had in mind when she'd been so flippant about the lack of danger. As far as she was concerned, letting Gray sit too close to her was far more risky than sharing her space with some innocent insect. Or even with a poisonous one.

Before she could promise to find him his own safe spot, he'd plopped down beside her with a sigh.

"Boy, I can see it's time I went back to jogging," he groaned. "That run really wore me out."

"The stress of worrying about Missy made everything more difficult. You kept up better than most." A lightning flash illuminated his smile and gave Stacy the impression he was aglow with pride.

"Hey, thanks."

"You're welcome. Just don't let it go to your head." Loosening the chest strap on her pack she started to slip it off her shoulders. When Gray reached to help her, she said, "I can do it."

"I know you can. The fearless Stacy Lucas can do anything. Alone. Unaided. And better than most men. But give me a thrill. Let me help you a little, will you?"

Even in the darkened cave there was enough light from the ongoing storm for her to see his face. It was like watching a scene illuminated by an irregularly pulsing strobe light. And every time there was a flash, Gray's grin looked wider, more self-satisfied.

Together, they freed her arms. Stacy laid the pack behind her. "You don't have to be so smug. I never said I was invincible or infallible. If I were, I'd have recharged the batteries in my cell phone."

"You're close to infallible," he countered. "Have you always been so self-reliant?"

She stretched her arms over her head to soothe her taut muscles, then shook her head. "No. When my parents died, I was a basket case. Couldn't even think, let alone function. I had one aunt but she and her husband traveled all the time and they didn't want me.''

"What happened then?''

"Oh, nothing much. A succession of foster homes. A reputation for running away.'' She took a deep, settling breath. "Are you sure you want to hear all this?''

"Positive.''

"Okay. But my life isn't very interesting until I get to the part where I came to Jesus.'' Stacy could see that he was paying close attention so she went on. "I must have been about fourteen. Thought I knew all there was to know about life—which of course is a joke.''

"We all think we're smarter than anyone else at that age. I did, too,'' he said.

"True. But in my case, I proved how dumb I was. I packed as many belongings as I could carry, hitched a ride to Utah—of all places—and got lost in the Wasatch Mountains. I'd have died of dehydration and hypothermia if it hadn't been for a search team...with dogs.''

Gray saw her shudder. "Are you cold, now?''

"No. Just thinking. I'd already been alone for nearly four years when I headed for Utah. I was pretty scared and hungry by the time I realized I was in real trouble. That was when the miracle happened.''

He sat up straighter, leaned closer. "Go on.''

"You're going to think I'm crazy," Stacy warned.

"Let me be the judge of that."

"Okay." Nodding, she allowed the bittersweet memories to flood her mind, fill her heart. "I'd prayed hard after the plane crash that Mommy and Daddy would be all right. When I was told they'd both died, I was furious with God. I gave up any remnants of faith I might have had left over from my earlier days in Sunday school.

"Then, up in the Wasatch, when I honestly thought I was going to die, I suddenly thought of Jesus. I didn't know why, then, and I don't have a clue now, either. I was crying my eyes out and babbling incoherently. Somewhere, in the midst of all that hysteria, was a plea for rescue. I do recall telling God that I was sorry and that if He wanted me, He could have me."

Stacy smiled over at her companion. "The rest is history. I knew He accepted me. Just as I was. Messed up. Useless. A total failure with a reputation for being incorrigible."

There was a catch in Gray's throat. "That's when the rescuers with the dogs found you." It wasn't a question.

"Yes."

"That's amazing."

"There's more. You see, nobody knew I was lost. The search party that saved me had been sent out to look for a missing hiker." Her countenance glowed from the retelling of the tale. "And they came across me first. I believe the Lord directed them."

"Wow. That does sound like a miracle."

"I thought so." Staring out into the storm she drew up her knees and wrapped both arms around them. After a brief silence she added, "I still do."

The temperature dropped rapidly when the cold front arrived to displace the stifling heat. Hail gave way to torrential rain. Still damp from perspiring less than half an hour before, Stacy rubbed her upper arms. "I think you'd better check on Missy. She's probably cold."

"I put my jacket over her the last time I got up," Gray said. "She's fine." He scooted closer to Stacy and laid his arm gently around her shoulders.

She stiffened and inched away. "Don't bother about me. I'm not chilly."

"Well, I am. We can't light a fire because we don't have any dry wood, and I know your dog won't let me hug him to keep from freezing to death, so that leaves you."

Disbelief was quickly replaced by embarrassment when she looked over at Gray and realized he was telling the truth. His clammy shirt was stuck to his chest. Goose bumps dotted his bare forearms. And he'd given up his jacket to keep Missy warm, which really was sweet of him.

When he shivered, she gave in and repositioned

herself by his side. "Okay. But no funny business. I'm only doing this because I feel sorry for you."

Gray wrapped her in his embrace, smiled, and pulled her closer. "Yes, ma'am. I'll remember that." His hand pressed her cheek and urged her to lean her head against his chest. "You sleep a bit, then I will. It'll be morning soon and we can start back."

Not nearly soon enough for her, Stacy thought. She could hear the steady beating of Gray's heart, sense the runaway hammering of her own in response. Yet, allowing him to watch over her, even for a short while, gave her an unexplainable feeling of peace. On the other hand, she also had the urge to jump up and escape his clutches, no matter how illogical the idea was under the present circumstances.

Disgusted, she made a face. There was nothing to worry about. She'd have plenty of opportunities to distance herself from Graydon Payne once they returned to civilization. *Sure she would.* She could join the foreign legion. Or become a missionary and volunteer to go to Africa. That should be far enough away to keep him out of her hair.

Well, almost.

She yawned, snuggled closer and rested her palm on his chest. Exhaustion overcame her. It felt so good, so safe, to be cuddling in his warm, strong embrace while the horrible storm raged outside. It couldn't hurt to relax and enjoy the experience a little, as long as Gray didn't know how much she liked being in his arms.

Closing her eyes, Stacy let her imagination carry her. In her musings, Gray was holding her because he loved her the same way she loved him. His family was transformed into one as loving and kind as hers had been. And Mark and Candace became the perfect parents for Missy, loving her the way Stacy had once prayed to be loved when she was young and alone, too.

It was a perfect world. A perfect dream. Cherishing those perceptions, holding on to them as long as she could, she slipped into peaceful slumber.

Gray felt her relaxing. He tightened his embrace. As soon as he was sure she was asleep, he placed a tender kiss on the top of her head and murmured, "We have to quit meeting like this. It's too hard on me."

Not that any other time they'd been together was any easier. Treating Stacy to the casual cookout hadn't broken down the unseen barriers between them nearly as well as he'd hoped. He'd been sure it would help her see that they could breach the colossal chasm between their respective lives if they wanted to badly enough.

Pensive, he sighed. Maybe he'd been expecting too much. After all, it wasn't just the past that separated them. The present did, too. He knew Stacy wanted no more to do with the kind of life he lived than she did with his family. Which was another big problem. They might be hard to take—they *were* hard to take. Nevertheless, they were still his family. Nathan wasn't an openly loving man but he'd married Estelle when he knew she was already expecting. That had to count for something. Even if the man hadn't been able to love his first son the way he'd loved Mark, he'd at least provided for them equally.

Gray closed his eyes. Thank God for James's friendship and spiritual influence. Without that, Nathan's emotional rejection might have soured him on everything and permanently ruined his life.

"Thank you, Jesus," he whispered. "For bringing me through."

Stacy took a deep breath and released it as a sigh. The hand resting on Gray's chest moved in a slight caress.

He held motionless. Listening to her slow, even breathing he decided she was still asleep. Which meant she didn't know what she was doing.

Snorting in self-derision he realized that he didn't know what he was doing, either. Or why he was doing it. And he was wide-awake!

"Please, Father," Gray prayed fervently. "Guide me so nobody gets hurt. Especially not Stacy."

He began to slowly rock back and forth, cradling her gently, lovingly, and adding a heartful of wordless pleas to his spoken request.

It was almost dawn before he dozed.

Chapter Fourteen

Missy stirred when her canine pillow got up, stretched with a yawn and sauntered outside to bask in the early morning sun that had begun to filter through the trees.

The child's whimper startled Gray awake. He blinked rapidly, momentarily disoriented. To his surprise, he found himself slouched into an uncomfortable heap on a hard, rock floor, a backpack for a pillow. He was still holding Stacy Lucas. Even more disconcerting was the fact that she was hugging him, too!

He took mental inventory. It had been so long since he'd moved, his left arm was numb. The right one wasn't in much better shape. The rest of him was so sore from the prolonged contact with the unforgiving ground he wondered if he'd be able to stand, let alone extricate himself from Stacy's embrace.

He knew it would be easier on them both if he could get up and move away before she regained her senses. Stacy's arm lay across his chest so he lifted it slowly, gently, trying to ease out from under without disturbing her.

Instead of letting go, she tightened her grasp and snuggled against him with a sweetly murmured, "Umm."

Gray squirmed. Fidgeted. Tried to inch away. Stacy was going to be angry, and probably pretty embarrassed, if she awoke and found they'd wound up reclining against her pack. Together.

He felt her hold slacken. She stirred. He tensed. It was too late to escape. In spite of all his efforts to remain alert, for her sake, he'd dozed off sometime during the night. He was about to pay the penalty for doing so.

Stacy's eyes popped open. There was a white T-shirt beneath her cheek. A shirt that contained a warm, masculine chest; one she'd just been snuggling against! Scrambling away on all fours, she stared back at him.

Gray raised on one elbow and winced in pain. "Boy, I'm glad you finally moved. I think my arm died hours ago."

"What were you *doing?*"

"Keeping you warm," he said with a hopeful expression. "Or you were keeping me warm. I forget which."

Memories of the night and the storm tumbled through Stacy's sleep-dulled mind, then began to sort themselves out. She clambered to her feet and dusted herself off. "You're right. I—I'm sorry. When I woke up like that, I assumed the worst."

A lopsided grin lifted one corner of his mouth. Dark eyebrows arched. "Well…I didn't think it was *that* bad."

Stacy responded without stopping to consider that he was probably provoking her on purpose. "Well, *I* did! I hope you know I don't go around sleeping with strange men." Hands on her hips, she dared him to contradict her. Embarrassment colored her cheeks.

Slowly shaking his head, Gray stood. "I never thought of myself quite that way. A little different. Maybe even eccentric. But never strange." He stretched, yawned. "I'll have to have my public relations people check on that when I get back to the office."

He started for the door of the cave. "Give me five minutes, then I'll gather up our stuff and get ready to go while you take care of Missy."

Dumbfounded, Stacy watched him disappear into the forest. A public relations department? Did he really have one? Probably. She knew so little about his business that almost anything was possible. In spite of all they'd been through together, all they'd talked about, he'd never shared that part of his life.

She shrugged. Did it really matter? Yes, it did. If Gray had been getting serious about her, the way she'd hoped, he'd have wanted to tell her about his work, to share the other important elements in his life, whatever they were. In truth, Missy's continuing disobedience was the only reason they were together. If Stacy hoped to hang on to even a tiny piece of her heart, she'd better put a stop to it. Soon.

Before she could change her mind, she crossed to where the girl sat, whining, and dropped to her knees next to her, determined to be firm. "Okay. Listen to me, Missy, because this is the only time I'm going to say this and I wouldn't want you to get yourself into more trouble because you didn't pay attention."

"Where's Lewis?" Small, dirty fists rubbed the sleep from little eyes.

"Outside. So's your uncle," Stacy said. "You and I will go out in a minute. First, I want to tell you something very important."

The child pouted and refused to look up. Stacy lifted her chin so she'd be forced to meet her gaze. "Listen to me. Lewis and I *will not* come looking for you again. Ever. Do you understand? I don't care how many more times you run away or where you go, we won't come."

Missy's lower lip trembled. "Why not?"

"Because it's not fair. At first, I thought you were causing trouble because you were unhappy living with Mark and Candace. I felt sorry for you. But that's not so anymore. You run away or hide just to make Lewis come and find you. Well, that trick is *not* going to work again, so you might as well knock it off."

The little girl's expression of pure misery tore at Stacy's heart, yet she didn't dare soften her approach. Not if she expected Missy to stop running away. Every time the child disappeared there was an increased chance she'd fall victim to a *real* tragedy. Stacy couldn't allow that to happen. She loved her too much.

There was also the matter of her personal predicament. Stacy loved Gray, too. She'd fallen for him against all odds and now she was going to have to make a clean break. Missy's obedience was the key to doing that successfully.

Unrequited love had already driven Stacy to the point where she'd actually toyed with the idea of giving up the job she knew the Lord had blessed her with. A career-wrecking attitude like that was so unacceptable it scared her.

Missy had begun to cry. "Please, Stacy, don't be mean to me. I love Lewis."

Deeply moved, Stacy reached for Missy's hand. Deciding what she ought to do had been easy compared to doing it. She knew she should tell the little girl she didn't care about her. That she didn't ever want to see her again. She simply couldn't speak those hurtful words.

The small hand gripped hers with complete trust. When Missy said, "I love you, too, Stacy," there was no going back. Moisture filled Stacy's eyes. Her heart overflowed with compassion. She took

Missy in her arms. This child's innocent love was not going to be rejected the way hers had been so many times.

"I love you, too, Missy," she said as tears slid silently down her cheeks. "Very much. That's why I want you to promise me you won't ever, ever run away again." She sniffled, holding the six-year-old away so their eyes could meet. "Promise?"

Missy nodded solemnly. "Don't cry, Stacy. I promise."

Pulling her close again, Stacy kissed the grimy little tear-streaked cheek without hesitation. "Good. I believe you mean that. I'm going to trust you to keep your word."

"Will I get to see Lewis and the puppies? I asked Jesus if I could, too. Was that okay?"

Closing her eyes and drawing a deep, settling breath, Stacy surrendered. She knew what the Lord wanted her to say. What was more important, her own peace of mind or the love and trust of an innocent child? She couldn't put herself first when Missy's future might depend on finding someone—or something—to love and accept her unconditionally.

"It was fine, Missy," she said softly. "I love Jesus, too, and I know he'd want us to stay friends, no matter what happens. I'll bring one of the puppies to visit you as soon as it's old enough to leave its mommy. Okay?"

"Okay!" Missy grinned through her tears. "Lewis, too?"

"Lewis, too." Stacy didn't know how she was going to manage such a challenging feat with all the opposition awaiting her at both Payne houses, but she'd think of something, even if it meant confronting everybody. The trick would be choosing a time to visit when Gray was elsewhere.

Emotionally overburdened, yet calm in the assurance she'd made the right decision, Stacy led the way out of the cave. Shading her eyes from the bright, rising sun she spotted Gray coming toward them. Her heart clenched.

He seemed weary until he looked up and saw her. Then the usual vigor returned to his steps. Stacy stood very still, watching him approach and taking in every detail of the poignant sight so she could store it away as a treasured memory. By the time he reached her, she was so moved she could hardly speak.

"Your turn," Gray said with a smile. He ducked into the cave as she and the little girl walked away, hand in hand.

His easy, unassuming manner, in view of her recent decision to stop seeing him, gave Stacy the strongest pang of loss she'd ever felt. And she'd felt plenty of others.

Where love was concerned, she was a regular pro at losing.

Stacy would have brooded if she hadn't had more pressing problems to occupy her mind. The winds that had brought the end of the storm had also toppled trees. The ravines they'd used as trails on their way out of camp were now filled with fast-flowing water. And the carpet of dead leaves on the forest floor was a slippery mess, making it much more dangerous, especially on a slope.

Beyond the natural obstacles there was an additional complication. For the first time since she'd gotten lost at fourteen, Stacy wasn't sure which way was home. Normally, she'd have simply radioed for assistance when she'd discovered her cell phone battery was dead, but they'd left the church camp in such a hurry she hadn't thought to assign her spare, short-range radio to anyone.

Slipping as she started up a soggy incline, she scrambled to right herself and paused to look back at her companions. Lewis had taken a place at the rear of the group. He plodded along, tail down instead of wagging. Missy was having trouble walking at all, let alone making decent progress. Gray had offered to carry her but she'd stubbornly declined.

"Stay down there," Stacy called. "All of you. I'm going to climb this ridge and see what I can see."

Gray shaded his eyes to peer up at her. "I knew we were wandering. You're lost, aren't you?"

"No." Her conscience intervened. "Well, not exactly. I'm just a little turned around, that's all. I'll get my bearings soon. It was the detours around all the fallen trees that confused me."

"There were only three of them," he countered.

"James is probably so worried he's called in the Marines by how." Frustration with the entire situation drove him to add, "What do you do in a *real* disaster?"

As far as Stacy was concerned, this *was* a real disaster. She was marooned in the forest with a grumpy man, a helpless child, and a weary old dog. Which meant she was everybody's best chance for survival. Except that she happened to be lost at the moment, a condition she was about to remedy.

Gray watched her climb. Every time her foot slipped or her balance wavered on the steep, rocky hillside, his breath caught and his irrational anger at himself built. He never should have let her go up there alone.

That ridiculous thought made him snort in self-derision. There was no way he could have stopped an obstinate woman like Stacy Lucas from doing anything, short of hog-tying her. And even then she'd probably have figured out a way to escape. She'd made a career of being a loner. Nothing he said or did was going to change that. He just wished he didn't care so much.

Breathless, Stacy reached the top of the ridge. From there she could see the aircraft warning beacon on the bell tower at the church camp. It was due south. All she had to do was figure out how to get them all there and her troubles would be over. Well, almost, she added, thinking of her promise to Missy and its ties to the Payne family.

"The cares of the day are sufficient," she quoted, knowing it was part of a scripture that dealt with not worrying ahead of time.

An ironic thought occurred to her. Here she was, lost and looking like a fool to the one person whose opinion mattered to her, and once again she'd failed to ask for divine help.

"Oh, Father," Stacy began. "I'll never learn, will I? I go around dealing with life on my own and mess it up over and over again, when you're right here, anytime I need you. What's wrong with me? Am I dense or something?" Deciding she was, she added, "Please, help me with that, too."

She was still talking to God and planning ahead as she started down the slope to lead her little party home. They'd have to circle the base of the hills and cut across a couple of low-lying fields. Happily, the trek wouldn't be as arduous as she'd feared. If all went well, in an hour or so they'd be close enough to the camp that they might even be spotted by the staff. After that, she'd just—

Stacy's heel hit an exceptionally slimy patch of moss clinging to a flat, rock ledge.

"Oh, nooo!" Her arms flailed. Both feet shot out from under her. Airborne, she had nothing to cling to, no way to stop her fall, so she drew in her limbs, protected her head and neck as best she could, and rolled with it.

Gray raced toward the base of the hill. If anything had happened to Stacy he'd—

Lewis shot past him in a blur, almost knocking him down. *Stupid dog!* He was liable to make things worse—if that was possible.

Stacy came to rest with a groan. Dizzy and groggy, she lay still for a few moments, taking inventory of her condition, then slowly sat up. Other than being covered with mud, leaves, and who-knows-what-else, she felt pretty good, considering.

Lewis was beside her, whining. "It's okay, boy. Don't worry. I'm fine." She wiped her hands on her hopelessly soiled jeans before reaching out to pet him. The look in his brown eyes told her there was something wrong.

Gray slid to a halt at her feet. "You okay?"

"I think so. But Lewis—"

"You slammed into him when you hit the bottom," Gray said. "I didn't like the way he fell. It looked awkward."

"Oh, no." Ignoring her own bumps and bruises, Stacy rolled to her knees and began to go over the dog gently, inch by inch. When she got to his right foreleg, he cried out and tried to rise.

She held him down. "No, Lewis. Stay. Stay. That's a good boy." Taking great care, she talked softly as she probed the sore leg, mostly to let the dog hear her calm voice. "It's probably broken. I can't be sure because it's not a compound fracture. The problem is, I can't let him walk anymore. If his leg is broken, putting weight on it can make it worse, even if I splint it first."

Gray hovered over her, his brow wrinkled in a worried scowl. "What do you plan to do?"

"Carry him," she said without hesitation.

His resounding, "Hah!" had so much force everyone else jumped. In the background, Missy started sniffling.

Gray reached out a helping hand to Stacy. "You haven't even tried to walk yourself yet. Can you get up?"

"Of course, I can." Rather than show how shaky she still was, she chose to accept his assistance.

He pulled her to her feet effortlessly, then quickly released his hold. "Okay. Prove it. Show me."

Determined to do just that, Stacy stood straight, set aside her temporary discomfort and took a step. The first one was fine. The second told her that the prior break in her thigh bone was acting up. In spite of her efforts to hide her distress, she favored that side. Judging by the way Gray was looking at her, he'd noticed.

"I'm fine. Really," Stacy insisted. "I limp sometimes because of an old injury. That has nothing to do with the fall I just took."

"Missy told me about your leg. How badly does it hurt?"

"It's just a little stiff, that's all."

"Right."

Clearly, he doubted her ability to handle Lewis by herself. Truth to tell, Stacy agreed with him.

The strained muscles in her leg were killing her. And Lewis was no lap dog. He weighed at least sixty pounds. He was also in misery, which meant she'd have to take care not to jostle him too much. It was going to be a long walk back to camp unless she could persuade Gray to do things her way.

"I'll stay here with Lewis while you and Missy go on," Stacy said firmly. "When you get back to the camp, you can send help. It isn't far. I'll draw you a map. I know for sure where we are now."

Gray wasn't convinced. "What if Missy and I got lost? Or weren't able to find you again? What would you do then?"

"Probably give up and pray, which is what I should have done already," she said cynically.

"Not a bad idea. However, I happen to believe that God also expects us to make sensible choices in the first place. I don't assume He'll bail me out of every stupid predicament I get myself into. Neither should you."

Stacy was incredulous. "You think that's what I do? Okay. Like what?"

"Oh, like refusing to admit when you were lost. Or leaving the camp without arranging for radio contact first." He half smiled. "Or getting steamed at me for falling asleep in the cave last night, even though I behaved myself."

He would have to rub it in, and with a know-it-all smile, to boot. Stacy was at the end of her rope. "Listen, mister. My favorite dog is hurt, my leg is killing me and I'm stuck in the wilderness with you and the cause of all this. The only mistake I made was coming here in the first place. I've already warned Missy and now I'm telling you. Don't call me anymore. I won't be available and neither will Lewis. Period. Got that?''

''Got it,'' he said, feigning indifference. ''Now, if you're through lecturing me, splint the dog's leg and let's all get going. I'm not about to spend another night here.''

''Well, at least I have *that* to be thankful for,'' she muttered under her breath. Choosing a straight, sturdy stick she bound it to Lewis's leg with gauze from the first-aid kit in her pack.

As soon as the doctoring was done, Missy caressed the old dog's head and leaned close to whisper in his ear. ''Don't worry, Lewis. I'll get you a special treat.'' She grinned. ''I know. Ice cream! Would you like that? I'll bet you would, 'cause I know we both love the same stuff.''

Giggling, she peeked up at Stacy, then looked from her to the man who was standing close by. ''You should be nice to Uncle Gray, too, you know. He's my bestest friend.'' She quickly added, ''Besides you, Lewis. I love you bunches.''

Gray was fighting the strong urge to scoop Stacy up in his arms and carry her all the way back to camp, regardless of the indignation he knew he'd face if he dared suggest it. It distressed him greatly to see her favoring her leg and trying to cover up the obvious pain. If she tried to tote that monster of a dog, the way she'd vowed she would, he knew she'd never make it. And she'd hurt herself trying because she'd be too hardheaded to admit defeat.

That conclusion left him no choice. As soon as Stacy hefted her pack, he said, "You carry that. I'll bring the dog."

Wide-eyed, she stared at him. "You're kidding."

"Not about something as serious as that. I'm the logical one, remember? I insist."

"Why? Because you think I can't do it?"

"No. Because Missy's too small and you're needed to lead us out of here. Besides, the dog deserves somebody who can carry him with the least amount of suffering. Me."

"Oh? Well, what if he decides to bite you when you pick him up?"

"Believe me, I've thought of that. I have the feeling he'll accept my help. He's quit growling at me every time I go near you or Missy, so he must have mellowed some."

"He's also hurt," Stacy reminded him. "That will make him less predictable."

Like his mistress, Gray mused. "Well, we won't know unless we try, will we?" Moving slowly, purposefully, he approached the place where his niece comforted the dog.

"It's okay, Uncle Gray," the girl said. "I told Lewis to like you."

"Oh, good. Did he listen?"

"Uh-huh. He's a good boy." She leaned down

to plant a wet kiss on his furry, golden cheek. "Aren't you, Lewis?"

Gray was encouraged to see the dog's tail thump the ground. He spoke aside to Stacy. "I think it'll be best if you help me lift him so he knows it's okay with you. If we're going to have any trouble, it'll probably be when we first move him."

"I agree."

Approaching, she edged Missy out of the way and took her place, speaking in sugary tones. "Okay, Lewis, now be good. Mr. Payne is going to pick you up and I don't want you to take a piece out of him. At least not until we're back in civilization. Okay?"

"Oh, that was sweet," he remarked. "Thanks a heap."

"You're welcome." If Stacy hadn't been so worried about the dog, she'd have chuckled. "I'll lift his head and neck," she said. "You slide your arms under his body. It'll be easier to carry him if you support the middle and let both ends hang loose."

Gray did as he was told. Coordinating his efforts with Stacy's, he straightened while she continued to murmur calm reassurances to Lewis. The animal obviously trusted her completely. Hopefully, some of that trust had rubbed off on him. There was only one way to find out.

"Okay. Let go," Gray ordered. "Back off. Let's see what he does."

Nodding, Stacy released her hold. Lewis immediately swiveled his head to look up at the man who still held him. Before Stacy could intervene, the dog's broad tongue shot out to give Gray's face an amiable slurp! Missy giggled.

Gray realized he'd been holding his breath. "Whew! He had me worried when he looked at me like that. I was already planning what I'd tell the emergency room doctor."

Temporarily speechless and trying to recover from Lewis's surprising change of heart, Stacy just stared. Since she and Gray had been at odds so often, she'd assumed the dog's attitude would reflect that mood. It was a real shock to find that it didn't.

She pulled a face as she shouldered her pack. What a disgusting development.

Clearly, Lewis had defected.

Chapter Fifteen

Gray'd had trouble negotiating the thick forest without jostling Lewis's injured leg. Now that they were on flatter ground he was starting to feel more confident, even though his arms were about to give out. "I told James to give us till noon today before he called for a full search. Think we might get there in time to stop him?"

Stacy looked at her watch, then at him. "Almost. How are you holding up?"

"I'm hanging in there. I wouldn't have believed this dog was so heavy by looking at him."

"He's solid muscle, even at his age. I keep all my dogs in top condition." Her smile was demure but condescending. "Maybe you should start working out with them."

Gray refused to take the bait. "Not if I have to eat kibble and sleep outside on the ground. I've had enough roughing it to last me a lifetime, thank you.''

He plodded past her, noting how refreshed she looked compared to the way he felt. There must be some way to get a little relief. Maybe it would be easier if he carried Lewis on his back. It wouldn't hurt to ask if that was feasible. ''Have you ever considered making a sling for injured dogs so you could lug them like a backpack?''

''No. But that's a good idea.'' Stacy studied man and dog. ''We can try draping him over your shoulders, if you like. I can't see why it wouldn't be as good as the way you're carrying him now, as long as you didn't have to hold on to his sore leg to balance him.''

''And we might make better time that way.''

''Yes.'' Her voice was devoid of emotion, reflecting the numbness she was feeling. Helping him reposition the injured dog for ease of transportation, she bit back tears of regret. Above all, Gray must never suspect how much she cared for him, or how desperately she'd miss him when they no longer had reason to see each other.

Sorry for the way she'd had to intimidate the child to make her promise to behave, Stacy salved her conscience by asking, ''What do you think about my giving Missy a puppy? Would Candace and Mark permit it?''

''You'd have to ask them.''

''Oh, *that* should be fun,'' Stacy retorted. ''Almost as much fun as being thrown out of your father's house as soon as he didn't need me anymore.'' She immediately realized she was being overly defensive and added, ''Sorry. I shouldn't have said that.''

''Dad didn't throw you out.''

''Oh, no? He sure didn't invite me to stay for tea!''

Gray had to admit that was true. Unfortunate, but true. He was so used to the way his family behaved he'd laughed off the incident. Obviously, Stacy hadn't. ''My father's not the friendliest guy in the world but he's good to my mother. And he supports several charities very generously.''

''How nice.'' What a shame that the Paynes considered their conduct normal, she thought. Why couldn't they see how much happier they'd be if they expressed a little Christian love and compassion once in a while and stopped being so judgmental toward anyone who was different from them?

That line of reasoning brought Stacy up short. *Oh, boy!* It took one to know one, didn't it? Her pace slowed. Her conscience twisted. All the family counselors in the world wouldn't do a bit of good unless a person sincerely wanted to change for the better. She had Christ in her heart, yet she was still judging people negatively. If she couldn't be as loving as she should be, with all that divine help, what chance of genuine reform did a family like Gray's have?

Her heart sank as she accepted the truth and

sought a remedy. If she could pray for the Paynes—and really mean it—maybe she could finally relinquish the animosity in her own heart. That change could make all the difference in the world when she approached them about Missy's puppy. She might not be able to put *all* of her old resentment aside, but it was worth a try.

She owed it to a lonely little girl to do her best.

James and a team of other able-bodied men met Stacy's party a quarter mile from the camp border. Lewis didn't object when Gray handed him off to two of them.

"Whew! I've never been so glad to see anybody in my life," Gray told James. Together, they watched Stacy and Missy go on ahead, flanking the men who now carried Lewis. "That dog weighs a ton."

James clapped him on the back. "Glad to see you, too, buddy. You had me worried."

"Yeah. Me, too." Gray motioned his friend aside and plopped down on a fallen log to rest and catch his breath. Finally, he said, "Missy found us a cave just before the storm hit. She's quite a kid. I just wish I could be sure she was eventually going to settle down."

"Which reminds me," James said. "Your brother called while you were gone."

Gray stiffened. "You didn't tell him Missy had taken off again, did you?"

"No. But he did leave you a message."

The look on James's face made the hair at the back of Gray's neck prickle. "I'm not going to like this, am I?"

"I doubt it. Candace is pregnant. Mark said to tell you he's calling off the adoption."

"No! He can't. It'll destroy Missy." Not to mention what would happen to his own emotional state, he added silently. "And Stacy will be livid. She's identified so closely with Missy she'll be sure to blame my whole family."

"What can *you* do about it?"

"I don't know." Gray got to his feet and began pacing. "There has to be something. I can't let her be hurt."

"Who are we talking about here?" James asked wisely. "Missy or Stacy?"

That question brought Gray up short. He stared at his old friend for long seconds. If he were to be honest about his feelings, he'd have to say he loved them both. Huffing in self-derision, he started to smile wryly. "I think I'm in big trouble, here.

"I'd say so." James chuckled. "Of course, there is a logical solution. Marriage."

"Logical? Hah! You don't know the half of it. Stacy Lucas and I have absolutely nothing in common. It would never work."

"Who are you trying to convince? Me or yourself?"

"I don't have to convince anybody. It's a simple fact. She has her life-style and I have mine. She's made it perfectly clear that we're worlds apart."

"Okay." James shrugged nonchalantly. "What's stopping you from spending a little time in her world? I've been telling you for years that you should hire some eager college grads and let them take over some of your management accounts so you'd have more free time. Of course, if you're not really attracted to Stacy it would be foolish to marry her just to get a mother for Missy."

Gray didn't know what to say. Stacy was funny and fun, bright and sensitive, and her soul spoke to his like no one else's ever had. But there was more to it than that. He'd had a lifetime to come to understand what happened when people married for the wrong reasons.

"I have to tell you something," Gray said soberly. "I don't know who my real father was. It wasn't Nathan Payne." He was amazed to see that James didn't seem very surprised.

"I suppose that explains why you and Mark have such different coloring and features. And also why Nathan was always so ironhanded with you, while your little brother could get away with anything."

"How can you be so matter-of-fact about this? You know what news like that makes me."

"Who your father was, or wasn't, doesn't make a bit of difference," James said. "In case you haven't noticed, nobody on this earth is perfect. We'll never be worthy of God's love, any more than we're worthy of the love of a good woman like Stacy."

"She deserves better," Gray said quietly. "Somebody who knows his true background and can assure her there are no genetic risks or hidden pitfalls."

"If you're going to deny yourself a chance at happiness because you honestly believe that's what's best for Stacy, then I'm even more positive you're the right man for her. The question is, what are you going to do about it?"

"I don't have a clue. I guess the most important thing is to call my attorney and find out how hard it will be for me to adopt Missy."

"As a single man?" James probed. "Or a married one?"

Gray muttered under his breath. "Single. Unless God convinces me otherwise. Come on. I've got my second wind. Let's get started back." He noticed that his old friend kept his distance so he said, "I hope that doesn't upset you."

"Nope," James answered with a wry grin. "I just don't want to be standing too close when the Good Lord decides to reach down and zap some sense into you."

Stacy was getting into her truck when Gray reached the place where they'd left it the day before. The sight of her tied his gut in a knot of wishful longing. He couldn't just let her drive away without at least saying goodbye.

Her heart began to race when she saw him wave

and jog toward her. Maybe he was finally going to tell her what she wanted to hear; that he loved her and wanted to keep seeing her in spite of their differences. She held her breath. Hoping. Praying. Imagining how wonderful it would be if he took her in his arms and kissed her, again.

A broad grin lit her face as she greeted him. "Hi! I'm glad to see you've recovered." When he didn't return her smile, it waned. "What's wrong? Are you hurt?"

Not in the way you mean, he thought. He looked around. "Where's Missy?"

"The others took her back to the main camp to get her cleaned up and find her something warm to eat."

"I'm surprised she went with them, considering how fond she is of you and Lewis." He glanced into the truck where the dog was resting comfortably. "Is he all right?"

"He will be," Stacy said. She laid her hand on his arm to offer comfort. "But I'm not so sure about you? Are you okay?"

Gray sighed deeply. There was no easy way to tell her what Mark had decided. And his own thoughts were in such a muddle that even *he* didn't understand them, so how could he hope to explain anything to Stacy? Placing his hand over hers, he simply said, "Mark is calling off the adoption."

She jerked away. "What? He can't do that!"

"He's doing it. Candace is expecting a baby. That's the family they wanted in the first place."

"Terrific! How nice for them. What's going to happen to Missy? Or hadn't they thought about that?"

"I haven't talked to Mark about it yet," Gray said. "But Missy will be fine." He looked deeply into Stacy's eyes, waiting for her reaction when he said, "I'm going to adopt her myself."

"You're what? When did you decide that?"

"A few minutes ago." Gray raked his fingers through his hair, roughly combing it back. "I also thought—"

Stacy stared up at him. "What? You also thought what?"

"Never mind. It was a stupid idea. It would never work out." Part of him urged that he go ahead and tell her. Another part kept insisting it wasn't fair. He wished he was in a boardroom somewhere, making a professional proposal to a room full of hard-nosed executives. That would be *much* easier than talking one-on-one to Stacy.

"Suppose you let me decide if it was stupid," she said.

In a business situation he'd have had a prepared list of pros and cons to cite. In this case, he knew he cared too much for everyone involved to be nearly that lucid, so he decided to just plunge in. "Well, James thought maybe, since you and I both love Missy, we could get married and make a regular home for her." He saw a look of pure astonishment come over Stacy.

"*James* thought?" She couldn't keep her soul-deep disappointment from making her sound defensive. "But *you* think it's a stupid idea, right?"

"I have my reasons."

"I'll bet you do." Heartbroken, she turned away. Gray reached for her. She evaded his touch. Climbing into her truck she looked back at him only once before driving away.

He was standing there, mutely watching her go.

The break in Lewis's leg was a simple fracture, easily set with a lightweight cast. Stacy had waited at the vet's until the dog was ready to travel, then driven the rest of the way home slowly, so forlorn she hadn't even been tempted to eat the candy bar she'd found in the glove compartment.

When she'd run across the candy again it had reminded her of the last time she'd seen Gray. Of course, everything else did, too. She'd imagined she'd spotted him in her favorite grocery store. And driving down the street in neighboring Batesville. And even in church one Sunday. Each time she'd been wrong, and her usually sunny disposition had suffered terribly.

Onyx and Lewis's puppies were getting bigger by the day. Three of them were already sold and three more were going to experienced rescue personnel for training soon. That left only one. The one she'd chosen for Missy. It was a golden-colored female with big, beautiful brown eyes and the even temperament of its daddy. It also had an inquisitive nature that had been providing Stacy with hilarious diversion ever since she'd moved the pup into the house to be socialized and house-broken. Now it was time to deliver it. The only problem was, Stacy knew she'd probably have to face Graydon Payne to do it.

She hadn't been able to reach him at any of the places she'd tried, including both his homes. Finally, she'd had to give up long enough to drive into Little Rock to conduct a scheduled training seminar. Physically, she was there. Emotionally, she continued to agonize over not knowing for sure that Missy had found a real, permanent family.

Stacy's class was full, as usual. The students had been instructed to leave their dogs at home for the first session so there would be less distraction. She'd brought Lewis to illustrate the preliminaries because he was the most laid-back of her dogs, and because she was afraid he sensed that his working days were nearly over.

"Or maybe he's just picking up on *my* dumpy mood," she grumbled as she sorted through her notes and prepared to take roll. It was bad enough that she missed Gray so much her life had lost all its joy. It was even worse to know she was going to have to deal with him one more time before she was through. Add to that her ongoing concern for Missy's emotional well-being after Mark sent her away like an unwanted stray, and she had plenty of good reasons for being depressed. How could anybody do that to a child?

Someone laid a folder on Stacy's desk. Assuming it contained more enrollment forms, she added it to the stack. Suddenly, Lewis perked up, ears forward and alert, and thumped his tail on the floor at her feet.

Following the dog's line of sight Stacy did a double take. *Dear Lord,* she was imagining things again. The man standing off to one side at the back of the room looked exactly like Graydon Payne! She blinked to clear her head. The vision remained. This time, he was real!

Holding a beautiful bouquet of flowers he stood there, smiling confidently, as though he didn't remember a thing about his claim that marrying her was a stupid idea.

Stacy's first impulse was squeal with delight and run straight into his arms. Then she thought about how he hadn't even bothered to phone her since that day at the camp and she quickly regained her senses, acknowledging him with no more than a polite nod.

Gray stepped forward and pointed to the folder she'd just received. ''Tell me what you thought of that.''

Stacy never took her eyes off him. ''What is it?''

"A professional prospectus," he said. "I wanted you to know exactly what you were getting into before I asked you to marry me. Again. Look at it."

"Why should I need to?" She was having a terrible time remaining in full control of her wobbly knees and trembling hands, not to mention the flock of butterflies holding an impromptu square dance in her stomach.

He gestured again. "Because it's all in there. Every drawback and every asset. Read it. Please."

Stacy shook her head. "No. I do want to know about your work, eventually, but you're not going to get away with treating me like one of your clients. I want you to talk to me. If you have anything to say, say it."

He snorted in self-derision. "You mean here? Now?" The firm set to her jaw told him that was exactly what she wanted. "I don't know. I didn't do such a good job the first time I tried proposing."

"True. But since you've had practice, you should be a little better at it by now." She folded her arms across her chest and watched as the teasing tone of her comment brought a mischievous sparkle to his eyes, then added, "Since I love you so much it's making me crazy, you might start by telling me you're nuts about me, too."

There was a faint giggle from the back of the classroom. Closer to the front, somebody coughed, sounding like they were strangling on a repressed snicker. That was all it took to launch the entire class into giggles.

Circling the desk, Gray ignored everyone else and gently took Stacy's hands. "Oh, honey. I've been miserable without you. You're all I think about, all I dream about. But I was afraid that if you knew everything about me, you'd turn me down flat. I finally decided to do what I know best. I worked up a list of the pros and cons so you could make a rational decision."

Laughing and shaking her head, Stacy looked into his beloved face through a veil of happy tears. "There is nothing rational about my falling in love with you, Mr. Payne. I don't want to consider all the reasons I shouldn't marry you. I just want to follow my heart and do it."

"You do?" Elated, he swept her into his arms, kissed her solidly, and swung her around in a circle, taking care to avoid stepping on Lewis.

So overcome with gratitude to her Heavenly Father she could hardly think straight, Stacy held tight. As soon as Gray put her down she rested her palms on his chest, unmindful of their student audience, and looked into his cherished face. The spiritual rapport she found there blessed her beyond her fondest dreams. Only one important question remained. "What about Missy?"

"She's fine," he said, his expression filled with pure wonder. "She's already staying with me. I hired an older lady to look after her and they've become pals, so don't think I only came here to get her a mother. Okay?"

"It will be my pleasure to be her mother," Stacy murmured with tears of happiness running down her cheeks. "It ranks right up there with my delight at being your wife."

Loud applause filled the room. Stacy wrapped her arms around Gray and clung to him. Judy had been right. It was much better to know someone loved you and wanted to spend eternity with you, than it was to be alone. The only complication was that this intimate moment had come *now*.

Sniffling and grinning, Stacy let go of her future husband and stepped back. "I hate to say this, but I'm afraid I have a class to teach."

"No problem. I'll just take a seat right here in front." He quickly slid into an empty desk in the first row and faced her, smiling. "Go right ahead. Don't mind me. I've always wanted to learn how this is done anyway."

"You don't have to take my class to impress me."

"I know that." Gray's tone conveyed absolute sincerity. "I've been doing a lot of soul-searching lately, and I've realized it isn't enough for me to just work hard, then give my money to charity, the way Nathan does. I need to be there. To get personally involved with helping people. To be more like you...if you don't mind."

"No, I don't mind a bit." Absolute joy filled her to overflowing. If the good Lord threw any more blessings her way she was afraid she'd explode! Or dance. Or sing His praises at the top of her lungs. The way she felt right now, even if she did all three it wouldn't be *nearly* enough!

Epilogue

The white, clapboard country church was small, perfectly suited for the intimate wedding ceremony. James stood up as Gray's best man, paired with Stacy's friend Judy as maid of honor, much to that young woman's obvious pleasure.

Missy hadn't been able to decide which of her prospective parents she should accompany so she'd chosen to be a flower girl and walk bravely down the aisle by herself.

It was a balmy fall day; perfect in every way as far as Stacy was concerned. She'd been far more nervous planning her nuptials than she was taking part in them. Mostly, she'd worried that Gray would complain her arrangements were too unsophisticated or that her choice of a modest church was inappropriate. Her fears had proved groundless. He'd welcomed the simplicity with genuine relief.

As Stacy stood at the altar beside him and took her vows, she felt perfect peace, perfect love, filling the sanctuary. This was the very church where she'd declared her faith and this was the place where she was about to promise the rest of her life to the man she loved.

She glowed with happiness as Gray slipped the gold band on her finger. This time, she'd remembered to pray for guidance ahead of time and was trusting the Lord in all things. The fact that Gray's entire family had condescended to attend the wedding was one of the miraculous answers she'd received.

In addition, her entire tracking class had passed with honors, including Gray, and had all been invited. They, and close friends from church formed Stacy's substitute family.

Once this day is over, she thought with awe, I'll be part of a real family, again. Her heart swelled with so much divine praise she wanted to lift her arms and shout, *Thank you, Jesus!* right there in front of everybody.

Raising her veil and carefully folding it back, Gray prepared to kiss his new bride. Suddenly, several pagers squealed, startling everyone. Dozens of wedding guests scrambled to see if they were the ones being summoned.

"Oh, no," Stacy whispered. "Not now."

Gray was grinning down at her and shaking his head. "Don't look at me. I didn't bring mine." He ignored the slight tug on his left pant leg and tried once again to give his new wife the customary nuptial kiss.

The tug intensified. Missy's shrill, frantic little voice carried wonderfully in the small sanctuary. "I didn't do it, Uncle...Uncle Daddy! Honest, I didn't!"

Stacy giggled. "*What* did she call you?" In the background, the remaining guests started to laugh, too.

"It sounded like, *Uncle Daddy,*" he said in a hushed tone. He was barely able to keep a straight face as he crouched down to comfort the troubled child. "We know you didn't do anything wrong, Missy. Nobody's blaming you."

Reassured, the little girl solemnly whispered, "Okay."

"Good." Straightening, Gray slipped his arm around Stacy's waist then cocked his head toward the door. "Knowing you, I suppose you'd like to find out what the emergency is."

"Would you mind?"

"Not at all." Raising his hand to get everyone's attention, Gray announced, "If you'll all stay right where you are and excuse us for a minute, we'll be right back and take up where we left off."

Stacy glanced down. "You, too, Missy. Stay here with Aunt Judy. Okay?" As soon as the child nodded, she said, "Good girl," gathered a handful of the skirt of her floor-length, satin gown, and lifted it high so she could run without tripping.

Hurrying up the aisle beside Gray, she noticed

that most of their guests looked as though they thought the diversion was charming. To her added delight, even Nathan and Estelle Payne were smiling. *Would wonders never cease!*

The newlyweds reached the parking lot just as their paged guests were returning. "No problem," one man said. "Charlie's gone to take care of it." He began to frown and look puzzled. "Hey, what are you two doing out here?"

Laughing gaily, Stacy said, "It beats me. I was just standing there, getting married like any normal bride, and my groom started to run off. I figured if I didn't want him to get away, I'd better follow him."

"Now cut that out," Gray warned, "or I'll have to teach Missy to call you, Aunt Mommy."

"That was *so funny, Uncle Daddy*. I hope somebody got it on tape." Stacy's laughter heightened until her eyes were watering and she was gasping for breath.

Gray stood by and watched, unsure whether she was just very amused or on the verge of hysteria. "Are you okay?"

"I—I think I may—" she gulped in more air "—be a little more overstressed...than I thought."

"No kidding." Gray handed her his handkerchief before he put his arm around her. "Take nice, deep breaths and try to relax. You'll get through this. We both will."

Stacy rested her forehead against his chin and dabbed at her eyes. "Look at me. I never wear mascara. I let Judy talk me into using it today and now it's all over your hanky. I must look like a raccoon!'' She glanced up at him. ''What will your parents say?''

''With those two, there's no telling.'' He rolled his eyes. ''This morning, my mother blew me away when she told me my natural father has wanted to meet me for years. All I have to do is contact him when I'm ready.''

''Oh, Gray, that's wonderful!''

''There's more. She also said I was a lucky guy to have found such a wonderful wife.''

''She didn't!''

''Oh, yes, she did. And from the look I saw on my father's face a few minutes ago, I'd say he agrees. Frankly, I can't believe they're even here today.''

''I can,'' Stacy said. She dried the rest of her happy tears and gazed into her new husband's eyes, filled with empathy and love for the lonely child he'd once been.

''Why?'' His brow knit. ''I hope you didn't beg them to come.''

''Nope,'' she said, beaming. ''I prayed about it. Can you believe it? I actually took a problem to the Lord *before* I was knee-deep in it.''

Deeply touched, Gray clasped both her hands and drew them to his chest, over his heart. ''I'm so thankful for you. For what we've found, together.''

Stacy closed her eyes and whispered, ''Amen.''

*   *   *   *   *

Dear Reader,

The directions our lives take may sometimes seem random or at cross-purposes with what we think should happen. Yet, looking back we can often see that God was in charge of the circumstances all along.

For instance, my father was an immigrant. If he'd stayed in Norway, I wouldn't be here at all. My family moved from Ohio to California when I was twelve years old. I didn't want to go, but if they hadn't moved, I'd never have met and married my wonderful high school sweetheart. His job transferred him to a very small town where we raised our children in a country atmosphere. That prepared us for our eventual move to rural Arkansas and helped us fit in with our capable, hardworking neighbors.

Our married daughter once lived in college housing. In that same building complex, a fiction writing class was offered. If she hadn't lived there—at that very time—I wouldn't have signed up for that class and you wouldn't be reading this now!

Although I've repeatedly prayed about my career as an author and put it in God's hands, the road hasn't been smooth. There have been blind alleys and potholes along the way. I've taken a few wrong turns of my own making, too. But the Lord is faithful and here I am.

Now that this story is written and I'm beginning another, I leave it up to Him to speak to your heart and point out whatever this book contains that will bless you and direct you down the perfect path He has prepared for all believers. I hope you will "Trust in the Lord with all your heart and lean not unto your own understanding." He truly will direct your paths—if you let Him.

I'd love to hear from you. You can write to me at:

Valerie Hansen
P.O. Box 13
Glencoe, AR 72539-0013

Valerie Hansen

Next month from
Steeple Hill's
Love Inspired ™

A FAMILY IN THE MAKING

JUL   2000   by

Marcy Froemke

Jilted by her faithless fiancé, Brynn Weston is alone
and in desperate need of a job. She finds the perfect
position—as the nanny for architect Michael Hudson's
daughter. But he thinks she's just trying to catch a
husband. When she sees how much Michael and his
daughter need her help, she's determined to help them
rediscover their faith—in God and in each other.

**Don't miss
A FAMILY IN THE MAKING
On sale July 2000**

Love Inspired ®

Next month from
Steeple Hill's
Love Inspired ™

THE RELUCTANT HERO
by

Lenora Worth

When newswoman Stephanie Maguire is
attacked by thugs, the enigmatic Derek Kane
rescues her. Who is this Good Samaritan,
and why won't he agree to an interview?
Stephanie soon learns he's devoted his life
to doing good deeds. But why? Joining him
in his charitable work, Stephanie must fight
her growing attraction to Derek if she wants
to discover his secret....

**Don't miss
THE RELUCTANT HERO
On sale July 2000**

Love Inspired ®